Love Long Distance

Bill Bishop
Cathy Waldron

Love Long Distance

By
Bill Bishop & Cathy Waldron

Library of Congress Control Number: 2020914398

Paperback ISBN 978-1-7354250-0-9
Kindle ISBN 978-1-7354250-1-6
Hardcover ISBN 978-1-7354250-2-3

Book Cover Design: Cathy Waldron
                   Pam Marin-Kingsley

Stock Images: bigstockphoto.com
              stock.adobe.com

Dedicated to all brave
men and women who have
served in the military, and to
those who love them.

Acknowledgments

A BIG SALUTE to Jane Stucker for the professional line editing & proofreading, as well as amazing support and commitment. We are truly grateful for all of her hard work and dedication. We couldn't have done this without her!

We'd like to also give our sincere thanks to all of the many talented writers on FanStory.com who read the chapters of this novel as we wrote them, offering helpful suggestions and lots of encouragement. A special "SALUTE" to Laura Jan Lodle, an AWESOME writer there, and a dear friend to both of us. Her editing help and continuous support have been a blessing.

Thank you K.D. Mason for the back cover blurb. It's fantastic! Also, thank you Pam Marin-Kingsley for working with us on the cover art and for creating our book jacket. Great job!

Last, but certainly not least, we want to thank our readers. We are both "grinnin' like two possums eatin' a sweet potato" because we're thrilled to be presenting our first co-authored novel with y'all. We love writing together! It is also the first published book of Give a Salute! (www.giveasalute.com), our publishing company located in New Hampshire.

We know you'll enjoy this Smoky Mountain historical romance. Please consider writing a review or contacting us at giveasalute@gmail.com with your comments once you've read it. Your feedback is important and greatly appreciated.

Best wishes and God bless.

Respectfully,

Bill Bishop & Cathy Waldron

THE MEMORY OF YOU AND ME
~ To My Beautiful Mountain Man ~

Do you remember, when I was 21, and you were 23,
making sweet, passionate love under the willow tree?
On that cool February night, we held each other tight
beneath a blanket of starlight; ***it was ecstasy!***

Oh, can't you see how much I miss you?
How I wish you were here so I could kiss you?
But with a deep desire and obligation to fight
for our country, you did what you had to do.

Marching off to war, filled with faith and bravery,
leaving it unknown if you'd ever come back to me.
Now as days pass without you, forever I'll hold tight
to the memory of you and me—under the willow tree.

CHAPTER 1

~ GOODBYE ~

CATHY

I didn't want to let him go, but the train whistle blew, telling us it was time to part. The dreaded moment had come. Having said our vows earlier that day under the willow tree, we promised to always love and honor one another. Although an official wedding would have to wait, in our hearts we were now forever united.

"Commitment don't come from no piece of paper," Bill said. "It comes from how much we love each other, so don't let nobody tell you that we ain't married yet, 'cause we are."

Love Long Distance

After Bill boarded the train, he opened a window and bent down to kiss me. "I want our goodbye kiss to last forever, Darlin'!" he said. The tears started to flow. I couldn't believe this was happening. How could he be leaving me? I grabbed a hold of his hands and our fingers intertwined.

My heart ached in rhythm with the sound from the train as it started to clickety-clack along the tracks. I continued to cling to Bill, not wanting to let him go, but soon lost my grasp. "I can't live without you! I love you heart and soul!" I cried out. "Please Honey, promise you'll come back." Sadness, as bright as a firefly's light, glowed from his face as he blew me one last kiss.

"Of course I'll come back to you, Angel," he replied. "I'm a tough one, remember? And I love you heart and soul too. So dry those pretty eyes and don't ya cry no more! I'll write you all the time, you betcha! Before you know it, I'll be home."

I watched him depart, our eyes still fixed on each other, until he became a speck in the landscape. He vanished into the sunset, and I was left standing there alone. The man I loved so very much was headed off to war. I didn't want to think what the odds were he'd survive this journey. I bowed my head and said a prayer. *"Please God! Bring him safely home to me. Protect him until we can be together again."*

****

BILL

Clickety-Clack. The train started rollin' along the tracks. "Please forgive me, Darlin', but I must leave you now," I said. I had to be brave for both of us, so I tried to reassure her it would be alright, even though I wasn't so sure.

When I lost sight of her, I began to pray. I was angry at God for what was happenin'. *"Dear God! What have I ever done to deserve the iniquities You're dealin' me? Am I to wander in the darkness of hurt and sorrow, never to be with my soulmate in our tomorrows? Why load my shoulders with a cross I cannot carry up the hill? I can face the battles I must, and into You I put my faith and trust; yet my heart breaks like a glass fallin' on a rock when I think of leavin' Cathy all alone back home. I'm so mentally exhausted, Father."*

Love Long Distance

I dropped down onto the seat, my duffle bag on my lap. It contained the very few items I owned. Unzippin' the bag, I reached in and took out her picture. The tears started wellin' up in my eyes and that's when I remembered my grandpa tellin' me when I was a young'un that if I was gonna cry, I had to hide behind the barn so no one could see me.

I wiped the tears away quickly. The months ahead would be tough and rough. Although I didn't know if I was gonna make it out alive, I had to keep believin' we'd be together once again. Cathy was an angel, and we loved each other since the day we met last spring. She was visitin' her cousin in Pigeon Forge. I couldn't help but notice her walkin' down the street that one day, so I went up to her and asked her what her name was. She smiled at me—such an awesome smile—and when she responded, she made me laugh with that sexy New England accent of hers. Of course she laughed at my southern drawl as well. Was I worried about not bein' appealin' to her? Not a chance! I'm a good-lookin' guy with lots of charm. I knew she couldn't resist me.

"Goodnight, Beautiful," I whispered before puttin' her picture back in my duffle bag. I closed my eyes and kept rememberin'. It had been a long day, and there were many miles to go before we arrived at the base. The heaviness of exhaustion overtook me quickly, and I fell asleep to the continued sound of the train.

CHAPTER 2

~ MISSING YOU ~

February 10, 1964

Hi Honey,

I miss you so much already! I wake up every morning hoping for your usual call, only to remember it won't be coming. Why did this have to happen? Why did you have to enlist in the Air Force at a time like this? You've tried to reassure me you will be all right and will come back alive, but that's wishful thinking. You could die and then what would I do? The thought of living without you for the rest of my life is something I can't bear. You know, that's the crappy thing about finding one's true love—it's the crushing fear of losing them. I pray God keeps you safe and brings you home to me, because that's where you belong.

Many believe there's no such thing as love at first sight, but I know there is. I fell in love with you as soon as we met. When you came up and introduced yourself last summer, your smile melted my heart. Once looking into your blue eyes, I knew you were the man of my dreams. My heart squeezed, and I could feel my belly flip. Okay, I also heard that funny accent of yours and it made me laugh! I've grown accustomed to it, and now when I'm in my bed at night, longing for you, I can hear you whispering in my ear, flirting with me as you like to do.

We all gathered around the television set last night to watch the Beatles' first performance on the Ed Sullivan Show. As you know, there's been lots of hype about Paul,

Love Long Distance

John, George and Ringo, and this was the main event everyone had been waiting for. I heard on the news today that about 73 million people were tuned in. 73 MILLION! The girls in the audience started screaming and acting crazy even before the singing began. My cousin, Sue, was screaming along with them and getting all excited. I had been looking forward to seeing the Fab Four, but I was preoccupied with missing you. Every love song they sang made me miss you more. I began sobbing uncontrollably and my sadness was interfering with Sue's Beatles fascination. She nudged me hard and told me to stop it. When the show was over, Uncle Joe came over to me and gave me a hug. "It'll all be okay," he tried to assure me. Having served in WWII, he had to leave Aunt Betsy for a long stretch. They wrote back and forth to each other, like we're going to do. He said he doesn't care to recall many things about the war, but will always cherish the letters between them. They strengthened their love and helped get them through their separation. Oh I can't bear to think about us being apart for that long! God willing, our letters, faith and trust shall bond our "Love Long Distance." Our commitment to each other is such a strong chain. No earthly soul can break it.

As you know, I'll be heading back north next week. Without you here, there's no sense in me staying in Tennessee. It is best I return to New Hampshire and be close to family. My mom just had hip surgery, so I'll be able to help her some. I also plan on finding a job right away. Since I'll be staying with her, I'll have no rent to pay and will put most of the money I make into a passbook savings account for our future.

Today I was feeling down and out, so Aunt Betsy told me to do something creative to keep my mind off my sorrows. I tried to knit, but kept dropping a stitch. I finally gave up and did something else creative instead—I wrote you the following poem. Please keep it with you and read it when you are feeling blue. It will remind you that there's no such place as far away when

Love Long Distance

*it comes to our true love. For, within our hearts,
nothing can keep us apart. Just close your eyes
and you'll see me...*

CLOSE YOUR EYES

When your heart is heavy,
and you're feeling sad and blue,
just close your eyes and think of me
because I am here for you.

When I'm tired and trembling,
with hopes I cannot see,
I'll close my eyes; yes, you'll be there
to hold and comfort me.

Although our lives are far apart
in distance, all our days
are filled with love for one another
in oh, so many ways.

So when you're feeling sorry,
down a lonely street you go,
remember I am waiting here—
close your eyes and you will know

that I do so adore you
and what God joins never parts.
We will never be alone again
because He has merged our hearts.

Close your eyes and you will see me.
I'll close mine, then see you too.
Together we'll keep on dreaming
until all our dreams come true.

I can't wait to hear from you. You are in my thoughts all the time, and I pray for your protection. God Bless.

"ILLLYB!" (I Love, Love, Love You, Bill!)

Cathy

XOX

****

Love Long Distance

February 8, 1964

My Darlin' Cathy,

I arrived at Lackland Air Force Base in San Antonio, Texas this mornin' at sunrise. I'm sharin' this information because I want you to know what is happenin' here. The base is under the jurisdiction of the 802 Mission Support Group, Air Education and Training Command. It is also the only entry processing station for Basic Military Training.

We trainees live in rehabbed 2nd World War Barracks, 20-man capacity. Our beds are twin-sized metal cots with a thin mattress, pillow, sheets and blankets. Footlockers are made of a heavy-gauge vinyl, 30 inches long, 16 inches wide and 14 inches high. There is one at the foot of each cot, providin' storage space for clothin', gear, everyday items, etc.

Throughout my training here, and other specialized training ahead, a bed such as this is where I'll sleep and dream of you. So here I sit on my footlocker, head in hands, lovin' you, feelin' blue, and missin' you like a baby calf lost in the woods misses its momma's milk. While travelin' here on the train and listenin' to the "clickity-clack" of the wheels on the tracks, I wrote you a poem for Valentine's Day. I'm hopin' it gets to you before you head back home. The words walked outta my heart, on down to the pen in my hand, then came into bein'...

TAKE MY HAND
~To my Soulmate~

A resonant sound from above echoed
against my ears so clear, and God said,
"This is your soulmate, My son—
the most beautiful angel in Heaven.
I'm sending her down to walk with you."

"Although gorgeous with a fine mind,
at times she'll be baffled indeed by a
weed
pretending it's a flower, letting it grow,
undisturbed, up against the wall.
I know she always aims to please."

Love Long Distance

"She'll go into the beauty of a moonlit
night
to watch the weed flourish as you sleep.
Please wake up and go tell her,
'It's only a weed, Darlin'!'
Then pull it up and cast it away."

"Take her hand—I'm giving her to you.
Cherish her forever; it makes me happy
knowing you and she love one another.
Her heart beats only for you;
your souls perfectly match."

"A philosopher once declared true
'Things that are lost are all equal!'
But you know now,
beyond a shadow of doubt,
his words were false and unknowing."

"What would I do, Father, if I lost Cathy?
The air wouldn't move, nor the trees
grow.
I would miss the sweet scent of her
as the flowers would wither,
curl up...and die."

"My world would cease with no desire to
live
because I can't fathom a life without her.

Please tell me, God. I need to know—
would, in some way, You let her spirit stay
to comfort me as she did before?"

"Son, I say unto you, ask and your
soulmate will never leave your side; seek
happiness and ye will find it everywhere;
knock on the door of My Kingdom,
and it shall be opened unto you both."

Goodnight, Sweetheart. I must leave you now. I'll sleep with your picture close to my heart and whisper, "I Love You Long Distance!" Did you hear me—did ya, huh?

Our technical instructor just yelled, "Listen up, Heroes! Tomorrow's only heartbeats away. So off to bed—lights out!"

Gotta go...

"ILYHAS!" (I Love You Heart and Soul)

XOX

Bill

CHAPTER 3

~ GOD WILLIN' ~

February 27, 1964

Hi Honey,

I was excited to receive your letter before I traveled back to New Hampshire. I'm glad you are settled in, and I really enjoyed how you shared all the details of what it's like there. Please continue to do so—it means so much to me. I'm also glad you love and miss me too.

The cot you sleep on doesn't sound all that comfortable, so I offer you a suggestion: when you're having a hard time falling asleep at night, just imagine the two of us on the blanket under our favorite willow tree. With the branches hanging over us like a tent, you'll hold me tight, and we'll recite poetry to one another. Hmm . . . and how many kisses will you steal from me? Only the first one, because the others I'll give willingly! Oh Honey, I hope this bring you sweet dreams!

I can't stop reading the poem you wrote. It pulls at my heartstrings. Please don't you worry about ever losing me! I love you unconditionally, and will forever and ever. There'll come a day when we'll truly be under that willow tree once again, and guess what? I'll even let you have your way with me (and I don't mean just kisses!).

The past few weeks have been busy. That's good because I wouldn't have been able to bear them otherwise. Mom is doing well recuperating from her hip surgery. She has to stay off her feet and take it easy a little while longer, but she feels much better. Soon enough, she'll again be involved in all her church clubs and women's groups. Between her schedule and mine, I'll be lucky if I ever see her. For now, though, we are enjoying our time together. She knows I've grown attached to your family in Tennessee, and also knows that once you are out of that terrible war, we plan to settle down in Pigeon Forge.

She tries to hide it, but I'm sure she's afraid something bad will happen to you. I don't want to think about that! Every morning, noon and night I pray for your safety. God knows how much I love and need you. No, you're going to make it through, and we'll have a wonderful long life together. We'll grow red roses in the garden and walk hand-in-hand, marveling at the world with all of its beauty. We'll build our log cabin in the foothills of the Smoky Mountains as planned, and although we haven't much spoken about it yet, we'll also have plenty of kids. Okay, at least two, but if they look like you, I think we should have a dozen!

A couple of nights ago, Mom and I sat at the kitchen table eating popcorn and drinking Coca-Cola while listening to the Heavyweight Championship fight between Champ Sonny Liston and "Louisville Lip" Cassius Clay on her Sony transistor radio. I'm hoping you were also able to listen to it—it was so exciting! I had read earlier about Cassius Clay predicting he'd "float like a butterfly and sting like a bee." He said he'd knock Liston out in the eighth round and that gave him lots of attention. But who really believed he could? It was amazing when he did it in only seven rounds!

It's so lonely without you, Honey. At night I sleep with your picture beside my bed and hold tight the teddy bear you gave me. Remember one day last summer when we came out of the creek after swimming and there was a chill in the air? I was so cold, and you were too, but you took your shirt off and insisted I wear it over my bathing suit. I've since slept with it every night. I hold it up to my nose and breathe in the scent it still has of you.

Love Long Distance

Earlier today when I was headed to fill out a job application, I heard Buck Owen's new song, "My Heart Skips a Beat," for the first time. Such a beautiful love song; it brought tears to my eyes. All I could think of was how far away you are from me.

Well, it is almost midnight, and I really must get to sleep. Take care and always know how much I love you. I may cry tears of sadness because I miss you so very much, but I also cry tears of happiness for God joining our hearts forever.

All My Love,

Cathy

P.S. Sue stood in line for hours to buy some Beatles wallpaper. So crazy!

****

March 7, 1964

My Dearest Darlin',

The time has passed fast, like a greyhound dog on a race track. I'm on schedule with my training here at Lackland Air Force Base in San Antonio. I just have to tell ya that I've volunteered to enter the Air Force Commando Training with hopes of eventually leadin' a Special Forces Elite Joint Services Team.

Of course if all goes as planned, I'll be attendin' a Naval Explosive Ordnance School for 16 weeks, then a Joint Services Commando School for around 19 weeks. Once I've completed all of the training, I'll get a week's leave prior to bein' shipped over to Vietnam. Oh my God! I'm lookin' forward to holdin' you in my arms once again because I miss you and love you heart and soul.

Before you fall asleep tonight, here's somethin' I wanna say: you walk with a glow in your eyes, like a thousand fireflies in the night. The love in your heart is bigger than the Smoky Mountains. Your eyes tell me that you'll love me every day. No matter what may come, you'll be there to pick me up when I fall, and to chase the demons from my mind.

Oh yes! Love comes in blushin' colors of purple, orange, red, yellow, green and blue. Your love will always be what gets me through. You brought me sunshine when I only saw dark clouds and rain. You brought me laughter when I only felt sadness and pain. I'll be yours forever, I want you to know. So let's keep a walkin' over the rainbow. Heart-to-heart and hand-in-hand, we're sure to reach that promised land . . . where's there's a big ol' pot of gold waitin' for us!

Tomorrow is gonna be a challengin' day here. I've just been reassigned to an Elite Special Forces School, and it's as tough as Grandma's biscuits when Grandpa was foolin' around with her, and she forgot about them bein' in the oven. They almost burned. Are you blushin', Beautiful?

I'll dream of you tonight, hold your sexy body tight . . . and you know! Can't say it, Baby, because Grandma's listenin'.

Oh my! The little sheep are jumpin' the picket fence, and I've counted a whole score. But I gotta sleep now. However, I'll be back tomorrow night, and I'll count a whole lot more. Goodnight, Sweetheart. God Bless.

"ILYHAS!"

XOX

Bill

****

March 8, 1964

Hello again, Angel!

I haven't much time to write, but I wanted to tell you that we were on the firing range today. As our targets bounded from the ground, we fired until the barrels on our M-16 rifles almost melted down. Rat-a-tat-tat!

Another day without you, yet your wings keep touchin' my face. Although we're many miles apart, I can sense your sweet presence and hear the beat of your heart. I'll write to you again soon, Darlin'—God willin'!

"ILLLYC" (I Love, Love, Love You, Cathy)

XOX

Bill

CHAPTER 4

~ NO POPPIES, PLEASE ~

March 20, 1964

My Darlin',

I haven't heard from you in a while. Is there anythin' wrong, Beautiful? I love you more than there are bears in the Smoky Mountains and miss you like a fish misses the water in a dried-up pond. Although I'm busier than a hungry hog in a trough, I'm gonna take the time to tell ya what's happenin' with me.

I finished my training at Lackland Air Force Base in Texas on March 13th, and I'm now at the Naval Explosive Ordnance Disposal School at Eglin Air Force Base in

Fort Walton Beach, Florida. My training goes from March 20th to July 19th. If you wrote a recent letter, it'll be forwarded to me. My current mailing address is on the envelope.

Our training goal here at school is to become experts in rendering safe all types of weapons and ordnances, both conventional and unconventional, improvised, chemical, biological and nuclear. Occasionally we will perform underwater tasks to identify, service, and recover foreign and domestic weapons. We shall conduct demolition of all hazardous munitions, pyrotechnics, and retrograde explosives. Of course, we shall try and preserve our asses while performin' the tasks above.

It's bedtime now. The sergeant is flickin' the lights and demandin' us to get to sleep. I'll dream of you and whisper, "I love you long distance." Sweet dreams, Angel. I feel your wings touchin' my heart, and can hear you whisper back, "I love you, Honey!" I hope you are okay. Later . . .

Hi again, Darlin'!

It's the crack of dawn, and I have a little more time to write before mailin' this letter to you. I was exhausted and fell asleep quickly last night. I want to share the dream I had about my childhood in the Smoky Mountains of Tennessee.

It was a cold winter's night, and I was lost. I could feel my heart pumpin' like an oil well as I screamed, "Please! Will someone help me—I'm freezin'!" My nose and face were numbed by the blastin' wind. I tried movin', but the effort failed. "Oh my God! Does anyone hear me?" I cried.

Geez! All I could think of was what a waste for me to be freezin' to death so young when I had planned on doin' so much more.

Then I heard my grandpa say, "I've found Billy! Hurry and bring the lantern. I think he's still alive!" He started shovelin' snow off my body. After wrappin' me in a quilt, he carried me to the wagon, climbed aboard, slapped rawhide against the mules' behinds, and yelled, "Giddy-up!"

This actually happened to me when I was a kid. Did I ever tell you? I don't remember much about the ride home, except that those old mules were runnin' lickety-split. "They were haulin' ass!"

Once we got home, my grandpa hitched them to the rail, carried me inside, put me on a small cot in front of the fireplace, and yelled, "Take care of him, Grandma." He then headed out to get Doc Smith.

"Wake up, Commando!" The EOD Sergeant is bellowin' from across the room to me. He doesn't know I'm writin' to you from under the covers. Nuclear weapons training is in one hour, so gotta go. I hope I hear from you soon. Please don't go runnin' off with that good lookin' man down the street because it would break my heart. Hugs and Kisses! God Bless.

"ILYHAS!"

XOX

Bill

P.S. As you know, I always try my best at

anything I do. However in an hour, I'll be attempting to de-arm a live missile that did not detonate upon contact with the ground. Should I fail, you'll be notified by the Department of the Navy. Please remember, Beautiful, don't put poppies on my grave, okay?

****

March 19, 1964

Hi Honey,

I don't want you to get worried, but a couple of weeks ago, I was driving to town to get some groceries and was rear-ended. The impact then pushed my mom's Rambler into the car in front of me. My head jolted back, then forward, hitting the windshield. The rest of me slammed into the steering wheel. I suffered whiplash, a concussion, a few broken ribs, and also a broken nose. You should've seen me! Actually, I'm glad you didn't. I had two black eyes and my nose looked like Jimmy Durante's. Anyway, I'm doing fine now; the car is not. It's still in the repair shop.

I did write you while recuperating, and I gave the letter to my mom so she could mail it. However, I just found out she didn't. She claims that with all that's been going on, she forgot to, although I'm almost certain she never intended to. How can I prove this? I'm so damn mad at her!

Thank you for your recent letters and for loving me. As I read about you volunteering for Air Force Commando Training, I wasn't surprised. When I added up all the training time, though, it saddened me knowing that now it's probably going to be over nine months until I get to see you. How can I live without you for that long?

On a positive note, it's good that you won't be going to Vietnam for a while. It's hard knowing how much danger you'll be in when you get there. I even had an awful nightmare a couple of nights ago. You were injured in some way, and I could see your body on the ground. I tried to scream for help, but wasn't able to. I attempted to run to you, but my legs wouldn't move. It was terrifying! I woke up with my heart racing and then had a full-blown panic attack. Honey, I will always worry about you until you're here with me again.

Guess what? I received a call yesterday and was offered a job! It's a clerk's position at a local clothing store, and I start tomorrow. As soon as I found out about it, I went shopping there and bought a real pretty dress. It's blue and has raglan sleeves and a sailor collar. I also bought a pair of white gloves, some pointed toe flats, a pearl necklace and a pillbox hat. I think the outfit makes me look both professional and sophisticated, but I'm sure you'd flatter me by saying I look more like a movie star. Speaking of, would you believe that on March 15th, Elizabeth Taylor married Richard Burton? He's her fifth husband, and she's only 32. How many husbands is she going to go through? Honestly, she divorced Eddie Fisher less than *two weeks ago. Oh I'm sure these trivial things don't interest you, but you know I like reading about movie stars.*

I'm lying here in my bed as I write this. "Glad All Over," a new album by the Dave Clark Five, is playing on the record player. I'm wearing some cute little baby doll pajamas and know you'd enjoy the view. Oh how I wish you were here with me now.

The beautiful poetic words in your letters made my heart sing. I'm so blessed by your love. I thank God for bringing you into my life, too—you have filled it with so much happiness. Nothing can ever erase the many days we've already spent loving each other and, Lord willing, there'll be many more to come. You are my beautiful and strong Mountain Man. Yes, we will walk hand-in-hand to our pot of gold at the end of the rainbow! "You betcha!"

I should get some sleep now. It's already close to midnight and the new job begins at 9 a.m. I will dream of you tonight, as I always do. Although the miles keep us far apart, I hold your love here within my heart. You are always in my thoughts and in my prayers. God Bless.

"B+C=US!"

All My Love,

Cathy

P.S. Did you smell the scent of my perfume on this letter? I hope it makes you smile.

CHAPTER 5

~ COME HOME TO ME ~

April 6, 1964

Hi Honey,

Hey, where are you? Your last letter concerns me especially because there has been no word from you since. My mind keeps racing and imagining all sorts of dreadful things that may have happened to you! I hope it is just my imaginative mind, and your next letter is on its way.

Yesterday I came across a Kennedy half dollar. Some were issued this year and, apparently, are hard to come by, not just because of Kennedy, but also because of the silver. I put it in the ceramic Tennessee bank you gave me. Of course, it will always remind me of when we first heard the President had been shot last November. What a shock to the nation. Then to watch the funeral and little John Jr. saluting his dad's coffin . . . breaks my heart!

Speaking of deaths, I just found out that one of your heroes, Douglas MacArthur, died yesterday at the age of 84. I remember you telling me that he was a five-star general, best known for his command of allied forces in the Pacific theater during WWII. You also told me that he and his father were the first father and son to both be awarded the prestigious Medal of Honor. He lived a long and commendable life. God bless his soul.

I've got to tell you that I'm not doing so well here. I've started having panic attacks quite regularly since the accident and have no motivation to do anything productive. I was excited about the new job, but those uppity ladies that shop there are always gossiping and complaining. They just aren't my kind. As for Mom, she can get around fine on her own now and is getting on my nerves. I'm about ready to pack up and move back to Tennessee.

I know I have to stay upbeat for you, and I am trying, but it's important to share the hard times with you too. Please know that I am here for you also if you need to sound off about anything.

You are always in my thoughts and in my heart. Life apart from you is empty and gray. I share this in the following poem I wrote for you.

COME HOME TO ME

My world is empty, bleak and gray
because you are so far away.
My faith is wavering; distraught, I cry.
I'm lonely without you, I don't know why
it has to be this way—soulmates apart.
There's a constant aching in my heart.
You keep assuring me it won't be that
long,

but I'm having a hard time staying strong.

Uncertainties cloud up my mind.
I search for answers I cannot find.
Honey, I'm afraid of losing you.
I want to help; what can I do?
Disarming missiles, heading to war—
Will the hinges come off our future door?
"No poppies on my grave," you've said.
Please be safe—not among the dead!

I pray that you will win this fight.
Come what may; come what might.
Your body and mind remaining intact.
Bullets and bombs not to impact
the man who makes my dreams come
true.
Don't you know, I can't live without you!
I need you back with me to stay.
Alone, it's hard to face each day.

My world remains empty, bleak and gray
because you are so far away.
My body aches to be in your arms.
My soul, it longs for all of your charms.
I hope for you to come home to me.
Our plans together—will they ever be?
With us apart, I don't really know.
All I'm sure of is, "I love you so!"

Love Long Distance

Be sure not to doubt, I will always stay
true,
Whatever life brings or what we go
through,
there is no other who can take your
place—
your heart, your spirit, your beautiful
face.
Someday you'll hold me again close to
you,
and softly whisper, "I love you too!"
You know I'd wait ten thousand years
for you to kiss away my tears.

*I love you with all my heart and soul and
pray for you unceasingly. Please be careful in
your training. You're scaring me lately!*

"Hugs, Kisses, and YOU KNOW!"

All of My Love,

Cathy

XOX

P.S. If you see tear stains on this letter, it's because I've been doing a lot of crying. Oh how I wish we were back under the willow tree, together and without a care in the world — just you and me.

****

BILL

"De-arm the missile, Bill," I said to myself. Slowly, I cut the black and white wires—said a prayer, then cut the red one. The adrenaline was pumpin', and my heart was beatin' like the little drummer boy's drum. My hands were shakin', yet I was makin' an exit from the missile warhead. Suddenly, I lost my footing and fell on a jagged piece of sheet metal. The impact drove it deep into my stomach, I began bleedin' profusely, and darkness filled my eyes.

I wound up in the hospital emergency room and felt weak as a baby sheep. The gash in my belly hurt like hell, and I screamed inside my head, *"Why, God? Did You not hear my prayer back there?"*

Love Long Distance

"Is Bill going to make it, Doctor?" a nurse asked.

"Only God has the answer to that, Nurse," he replied. "He has lost a considerable amount of blood, his blood pressure is dropping, and I fear only a miracle will save his life now."

I was fading fast. "Sweet Jesus!" I was able to say, although it was just above a whisper. "Before I die, there's somethin' I gotta do. Please have someone get the poem in my left shirt pocket. I wrote it earlier today."

Luckily, the doctor heard me. "Quick, Nurse, his shirt is hanging up on that hook over there. Go check. He might be delusional."

"Although the shirt is badly stained and torn, it's here like he said."

"Great, now Bill, can you hear me? We've got it. Now what?"

"Thank you, Doc. Please read it to me. Then it has to get to Cathy, the most beautiful angel on Earth...and 'the love of my life.'"

Looking down at the poem, the doctor read it aloud.

Bill Bishop & Cathy Waldron

YESTERDAY'S GONE

Yesterday's gone; we live for tomorrow.
Not in years, months, or days. The clock
ticks away our happiness, bringin' sorrow.
Nothin' in life is guaranteed.

Geez! If we could walk back with pride;
become husband and wife; build us
our little log cabin on the mountainside,
never to be apart and alone again.

Sweet Jesus! We're whinin' like a dog.
I find it trite and trivial. Of course our
loneliness is heart-wrenchin'; a heavy log.
Sweet memories drift from my mind.

"Why, God? Why did You take the
pleasures
and joys we once knew? Soon, the
present
tense will be yesterday's buried treasure.
So, I humbly ask again, "Why, God?"

"Cathy and I are Your children; spirit souls
in earthly forms. We have no promise of
our stay beyond our next breath or goal
Tho' our hearts are one; forever and
ever."

Love Long Distance

~~~

"Quick, Nurse! Bring the oxygen. We're losing him!"

CHAPTER 6

~ HEART AND SOUL ~

CATHY

I was sound asleep in my mom's recliner when her black rotary phone rang. "Hello," I said into the mouth-piece.

"Hello, I'm callin' for Cathy, Ma'am."

"This is Cathy," I replied. "Who's this?"

"This is Billy's Grandpa."

"Grandpa! It's so good to hear from you. Are you calling because you miss me?" Hearing his voice made me smile.

"Of course I miss you. So does Grandma; I wish it were only that. Now, are you sittin' down? If not, please do."

The smile quickly left my face. Something was very wrong. *"OH MY GOD, please don't let him be dead."* No, he can't leave me!

"Sweetheart, are you there?"

I couldn't respond yet; I was trembling so. Tears were already streaming down my face.

"Yes, Grandpa," I finally answered, yet my voice was weak.

"I reckon it's been a while since you've heard from him," Grandpa replied. "There's good explainin' for this."

"No!" I slid off the chair onto the linoleum floor. I was afraid of what he was going to say next.

"He's alive. That's the good news, 'cept he's badly injured. That's the awful part. He had to have emergency surgery, and it's still touch and go. He's lost a lot of blood."

I was so choked up, I couldn't talk.

"Billy's mama was contacted earlier. It seems he fell against a sharp piece of sheet metal and it cut a large gash in his belly. They also hand delivered her a poem Billy wrote for you. I'll send it, but I'm gonna need your address."

"Grandpa, don't send it because I'm on my way down there. But . . . will you read it to me?"

"Why, of course I will, but forgive me if my voice cracks. It's quite an emotional poem, Cathy, and it came straight from his heart."

****

I sat a long time on the hard floor and cried my eyes out. I felt hopeless and alone. Mom came home, saw me, and asked what was wrong. Once I told her, she replied, "I knew something like this would happen. He's probably going to die."

Her comment angered me, but it also gave me the inner strength to stand up for myself, take hold of my emotions, and follow through with my plan of getting to Bill. Grandpa assured me that Bill's ma, who was already on her way to the hospital, would arrange to have visitation privileges extended to me. I was to get back to Tennessee, then Grandpa would take us the rest of the way. Although it would mean an additional eight hours to make the drive, he didn't want to travel alone there, nor did I. I stood up, wiped my tears, and looked straight into my mom's eyes. She knew I meant business.

Love Long Distance

"I'm leaving on a flight as soon as possible to get to his family home in Pigeon Forge, then we're headed to see him. Don't say another word, because I don't want to hear it! Bill is the love of my life and I'm going to be by his side."

She was speechless. As I walked away, I added, "I'm sorry, Mom. I know you care, but he means the world to me."

"I know," I heard her reply.

I left early the following morning. She didn't even say goodbye.

****

My flight on the TWA Boeing 707 seemed endless. I rested the best I could. It had been a long, sleepless night. I worried about how Bill was doing; I prayed that God would keep him alive. Usually in my most desperate hours, I'm compelled to write and so I did. The poem I composed comforted me some, and I planned to share it with Bill as soon as I could. *"God, please let me get there in time!"*

LOVE PREVAILS

There is nothing that can break apart
true love which lives within our hearts.
Though trials and tribulations reign,
not even death can unlink our chain.

Together, forever, through thick and thin,
we'll jump each hurdle, and we'll win.
So as we face our darkest night,
please stay strong and don't lose sight.

By the grace of God, we were meant to
be.
Joined at the hip, so His children may
see—
there's nothing that can break us apart,
for true love reigns within our hearts.

****

BILL

"Sweet Jesus! Why are you losin' me,
Doctor?" I tried speakin', yet could not hear
my voice. However, I well remember the

nurse strappin' the oxygen mask over my mouth as darkness filled my eyes.

Acceptin' my final earthly moment, I lifted my hands toward Heaven. With my left, I touched a vacant spot for my soul— and with my right hand, I touched the face of God. Quickly my vision became crystal clear, as I traveled back to review highlights of my life.

I nestle warmly within the security of my mother's arms. Always hungry, I eat ravenously and grow quickly.

Waddlin' on the sand, I build castles by the sea and shovel moats from one to the other. Sadly, I watch as the tide takes them away forever.

Hook-slidin' into second base, I'm called safe, stand tall, then bow to acknowledge the applause from my fans. Oh yes! I cross home plate a hero.

Acceptin' my diploma, I turn the tassel on my cap, and offer warm regards to classmates as they turn their own—one after the other.

Marchin' under the shadow of Ol' Glory, I pay homage to our fallen heroes as a bugler sounds Taps from across the hallowed grounds.

"Hurrah and Semper Fi," I yell.

Reflections of my life thereafter become mirror images as I lie on the hospital bed and wait for God to whisper, *"Welcome home, My son!"* Once again, like in the days of old, I laugh in a glad way.

****

"Wake up, Bill, you're having a bad dream! Do you recognize me?"

"Of course, Doctor! No one could forget an ugly face like yours. And as for my havin' a bad dream—no way! I'm still here today to say, "God ain't ready for me yet.""

"Geez! Until just now, I never saw a miracle happen. Are you in pain?"

"Of course, yet, 'No pain—no gain,' Grandpa once said. I have always remembered his words. Once I bit Cathy's lips kind of hard and she replied, 'That's not gaining you access to the rest.' As you know, there are times you win . . . and there are times you lose too!"

"That's it—I quit! What have I ever done to deserve caring for a flamboyant and histrionic Smoky Mountain man? Have you no mercy?"

"Golly, are you alright, Doctor? By the way, I'm the patient here!"

****

CATHY

As I walked off the plane, I saw Grandpa. He had aged a little in the past few months. When he saw me, he extended out his arms. I hurried towards him, letting him hug me tight, as I buried my head into his chest and began sobbing.

"Did Billy ever tell you that I'd send him behind the barn whenever he had to cry?" Grandpa asked. He kissed the top of my head and said, "Keep the faith, Sweetheart. He's a strong and determined man and loves you so very much. He'll do all he can to get through this. Now, let's get back home. Grandma is makin' us a nice meal before our travels to see Billy in the hospital. We'll get a good rest afterwards and be on the road early tomorrow, right after I milk the cows and feed the chickens."

****

Although I was upset, the aromas from Grandma's kitchen stirred up a healthy appetite. I enjoyed southern fried steak, mashed potatoes, hush puppies and buttermilk gravy and biscuits. As Bill would always say, *'Yummy, Yummy!'* While we sat on the porch afterwards, sipping coffee and enjoying some of Grandma's delicious cherry pie, Grandpa reminisced about Bill when he was young.

"He was always out explorin' and takin' chances. Why, I can recall when he was bitten by that rabid dog. You remember that, Grandma?"

"I sure do," she replied. "We thought we'd lost him then. Now we're afraid all over again; Jesus, Mary and Joseph, let him be alright!"

We all bowed our heads . . . and silently prayed.

CHAPTER 7

~ DEATH DO US PART ~

CATHY

*B*umpety-Bumpety-Bump. I listened to the noise transferring into Grandpa's 1951 Ford F1 Pickup as the tires rolled along the road. According to the map, the mileage from Pigeon Forge, Tennessee, to Eglin Air Force Base in Fort Walton Beach, Florida, was around 539 miles due south. The halfway point was Springville, Alabama. We stopped at a Union Oil Gasoline Pump there, and I noticed the price per gallon was 27 cents. I tried to give Grandpa a couple of my last dollars to help fill the tank, but he would have none of that.

Grandpa had driven for five hours nonstop, knowing we must get to Bill as soon as possible. We had passed by some beautiful areas along the way. I saw some nice homes and ranches and lots of rich farmland, yet I also saw many old wood homes, half-fallen to the ground. There were people inside looking at us through broken glass windows and cracks in the boards. I whispered to myself, "There but for the grace of God go I."

The road we were traveling had become rougher, with hairpin curves. I was not feeling so well and wondered if I could keep from getting sick before we arrived at the hospital. My tummy was upset, and I felt a dreaded tightness in my throat.

"Grandpa, how much farther before we stop and rest a bit?"

"Why? Do you need the ladies' room or somethin'?" He didn't need an answer once he looked at me. "Oh my God, why didn't you say somethin' earlier?" he remarked.

Grandpa immediately pulled off the road and cut the engine. He jumped out, then hurried around to open the passenger door for me. Not a second too soon. I barely had both feet on the ground when I lost it. Grandpa held my head in a soothing manner as I quickly disposed of all my breakfast.

"You'll be alright now, Cathy, but I gotta tell ya—when I looked over at you earlier, you were as green as peas in a pod," Grandpa remarked as he helped me back into my seat. Being so embarrassed, I still hadn't said a word. I knew my face was now red.

"Yes, I think I'm going to be all right now," I finally replied. "Please forgive me."

"Shucks, there ain't nothin' to forgive you for, Honey! Now don't you worry none, 'cause I've seen a whole lot worse in my lifetime."

Before starting up the truck again, Grandpa reached into the big chest pocket of his bib overalls, then extended his hand.

"Here's some dried mint leaves. Put 'em in your mouth, chew 'em, and be sure to swallow the juices. I may try to be tough and all, but I also get sick sometimes when I travel too far in this here ol' truck."

After that remark, Grandpa took a few more leaves, put them in his mouth, and started chewing. "Of course this truck is a might bit faster than my ol' blue mule," he said. Then he spit some leaves out of the open driver's side window.

****

Grandpa was right—chewing the mint leaves and swallowing the juices had helped. I already felt a whole lot better, and I knew we were almost there. I couldn't wait to see Bill, but was worried about what condition he'd be in. Would he even recognize me?

I could tell Grandpa was tired of driving, and he was also worried. To keep him going, I thought it might be best to engage him in some conversation.

"Grandpa, would you tell me another story about Bill when he was young? He's shared some memories with me, yet you know how flamboyant and flirty he is. We can never get to the end of a story before he's trying to kiss and make out with me." I started to turn red again. "Now, please, don't tell anyone, okay?"

"Hurrah, that's my Billy! He got those qualities from me, Cathy! Hey, I have a better thought. Rather than me tellin' you a story about him, why don't I let you read the one he wrote himself about bein' bitten by that rabid dog? He always loved to write and would use a paper tablet and #2 pencil when he did. Did you know that when he was 14, he won 1st place in a writin' contest at school?"

I didn't know! Why didn't Bill ever tell me? I glanced over at Grandpa and could see by the look on his face that he was thinking, in a happy way, back to those days.

"Billy did lots of writin' in this here truck travelin' along with me," he continued. "I still like to read his stories, and guess what? I have all of them in my old suitcase behind your seat 'cause I was readin' some last night before retirin'. I decided to bring them along. Thought it might cheer Billy up to read them also. Figured it might even inspire him to write more while he's there in the hospital." Grandpa cleared his throat, then spit again out the window. "That bein' said, why don't I pull off the road, fetch that story, and you can read it while we continue travelin'? Okay, Sweetheart?"

"That's a grand idea, Grandpa! I'm so glad you brought his writings along."

****

I listened intently to the sound of the ol' truck going *bumpety-bumpety-bump* as I

64

became lost in the majestic words in Bill's school composition book.

Written by Billy (age 16)
THE RABID DOG

"That dog is rabid! Get it away from me, Grandpa!"

"Wake up, Billy! You're havin' a nightmare."

"Then why did it seem so real? I could hear it growlin'; I saw it droolin' from the mouth and gettin' ready to leap. Why am I havin' nightmares —please tell me?"

"That's somethin' we'll ask Doctor Smith, okay? But in the meantime, Grandma has breakfast on the table. Now wash your hands and let's eat. Are you goin' to Youth Night at church later today?"

"Yes, Sir! That is if you and Grandma don't mind."

"Of course we don't mind. We're happy you want to. Be sure to take the coal-oil lantern and some matches. It gets pitch-dark on the old dirt road."

"So, the rabid dog was just a dream Bill had?" I asked Grandpa.

"Read on," he replied.

The day passed, and before long it was time to head out for church. Quickly fillin' the lantern with oil and my pocket with matches, I headed on my way. It was three miles from home to church, and I dearly loved the walk. Sometimes I made a game of tryin' to better my time each week.

Once I arrived at church, my friends and I gathered, as we always did, on the front steps to trade stories. As usual, the most excitin' thing that had happened to anyone, other than myself, was killin' a bird with their slingshot. When it was my turn to brag, I told them all about killin' an eight-point buck deer with my shotgun. I immediately became the hero throughout our county.

After braggin' some more, we attended Bible class. Then I said goodnight to my friends. It was now dark, so I fired up the lantern and began to head home. Of course tonight the shadow cast by my lantern was spookier, and it seemed as if somethin' was behind me. I heard hoof beats on the road ahead. Surely no one would be ridin' their mule in the pitch-black night without a lantern for light, would they? I stopped and waited as the hoof beats came closer and closer.

I quickly jumped clear of the road as an ol' silver mule trotted past, then disappeared into the night. Although I was guessin', I'd say it probably had leaped over a fence somewhere up the road and was lookin' for greener grass.

Takin' everything into account, I was still makin' good time on my journey home. As I approached the wood bridge, I heard the patter of dog feet and it gave me instant goosebumps. Was my nightmare from last night about to come true? Raisin' the lantern above my head, I saw the dog headin' straight towards me. Its tongue was swollen and saliva was foamin' around the mouth. "This dog's rabid!" I said to myself.

Faced with the reality of it all, I panicked and waited for the onslaught. "Get away!" I swung the lantern in front of me. The dog stopped on the bridge, bared its canines, and began to growl.

"It looks rabid, but it's not attackin'!" I thought. "Why not? Oh, I know! It's because of the flame from the lantern." Grandpa once told me, "Rabid dogs are afraid of fire and water." With that in mind, I lowered the lantern to my knees, took one step forward, and waved it back and forth. The dog whimpered and finally backed off. I tried to swallow, yet the fear hung in my throat. "Thanks for bein' right, Grandpa!" I whispered.

I slowly approached the dog while it continued across the bridge. It growled once again, then ran away...and so did I! I didn't stop runnin' until I got home and was safely inside.

Grandpa was sittin' in his rockin' chair in front of the fireplace. "For heaven's sake, Billy, calm down and tell me what happened out there."

"I'm sorry, Grandpa, but I met this rabid dog on the bridge and was so scared. I think it could've even followed me home."

Quickly gettin' his shotgun from above the fireplace, Grandpa headed out for the barn. That's because rabid dogs will attack the livestock. After about twenty minutes without findin' it, Grandpa came back inside and sat down again.

"Now tell me what really happened out there, Billy."

After calmin' down somewhat, I told my story. Then I did some homework before goin' to bed. I was happy that he believed me, although no one had reported seein' the dog, dead or alive. Could it have been a figment of my imagination? No, it wasn't!

I got bit by that same dog in broad daylight a couple of weeks later. Grandpa, Grandma and my ma were beside themselves with worry. They rushed me to the doctor where I had to get a rabies shot right away. We all thought I was gonna die.

****

"Oh my God! We've finally made it, Grandpa!"

"Of course we have. Although findin' a place to park this ol' truck was harder than haulin' moonshine whiskey in a Coca-Cola cup."

As we walked down the hall to Bill's room, I said, "Yay! We're only steps away. I can see his momma sitting at the foot of the hospital bed."

"Geez! Just look how exhausted she is, Cathy."

I quickly glanced down at my blouse and drainpipe jeans to make sure I was presentable. I also patted my head, hoping my Adorn Hair Spray had kept my new Sandra Dee hairstyle intact.

As we entered, I quickly ran to her, held her in my arms and said, "Bill's going to be all right, right? Please don't cry."

I looked next at Bill—the sadness on his face, the pain in his eyes. I dropped to my knees and cried, *"Please God! Send down a miracle to heal my soulmate."*

Bill's momma reached out to me, held my face in her hands, and then whispered, "God's awake now, Sweetheart. He heard your prayer up there, and He replied, *'No stronger love have I than for My children. And when they hurt and cry, I hurt and cry too! Although I work in strange ways, one day you shall understand why.'*"

Suddenly I felt my heart pounding and a tightness in my chest. I was getting weaker and weaker. I wanted to go to Bill and hug him tight, but instead I curled up on the floor . . . and there was nothing more. My world turned black.

CHAPTER 8

~ GRANDPA'S GENES ~

GRANDPA

Immediately sittin' up in bed, Billy stared at Cathy as she lay lifeless on the floor. Terror-stricken and weak from the loss of blood caused by the accidental sheet metal stabbin', he quickly pushed the alarm button attached by a clip to his hospital bedsheet. Just then, a blarin' noise sounded that would awaken a hibernatin' bear. Red lights began flashin', then Billy attempted to yell, "Doctor, Doctor, come quick! Please, help Cathy, because I think she's dyin'."

Billy's momma put her hands over her ears and said loudly, "All this noise, and

72

she's still not movin'! Do you think she's really dead?"

"Quiet!" I demanded. I can't believe the likes of you two! Cathy is gonna be fine. She just fainted—that's all. Poor thing was all stressed out about seein' her sweetheart."

I pulled my wallet out of the back pocket of my bib overalls and proceeded to calmly search through it. "Now I know I got one in here somewhere. Hmm . . . there it is!"

After grabbin' the small white object that looked like a padded suppository, I slid the wallet back into my pocket and knelt down next to her as my bones popped and creaked.

"Can you hear me?" I asked as I cradled her head in my large calloused hand. "Just breathe in deep now. This here will rouse ya."

Placin' the small white object right under Cathy's nose with my other hand, I counted to three. The strong ammonia smell penetrated her senses and her eyes popped open before I finished.

"Oh my! Where am I?" she asked groggily.

Love Long Distance

"You're in the hospital," I replied. "Slowly now. Let me get you back on your feet. Then I'll get you a chair to sit in."

At that moment, the nurse on duty came into the room. She could've won a beauty contest 'cause she looked just like Marilyn Monroe. She sashayed over to Billy's bedside, turned off the alarm, and said in such a stimulatin' way, "The doctor will be right here, but it looks like everything's all right now." Reaching for his hand, she gave it a squeeze.

Billy was now eyein' the nurse from head to toe and back again. Her big blue eyes batted at him a little too much for Cathy's likin'.

"You sure are a cutie!" the nurse said to him.

"Wow! Who are you? Someone new?" he asked, quite intrigued.

That did it! Not waitin' for any more of my help, and not carin' how weak she was, Cathy jumped to her feet and ran between them. She gave Billy a big hug, followed by a huge kiss. She wanted that pretty thing to know he was already taken.

"Oh Honey, I missed you so much," she purred.

"I missed you too, Beautiful! Now plant another one of those on me, okay?"

Before she did, she quickly turned back to the nurse. With a look that could kill a mockingbird, Cathy said to her, "Yes, everything's okay, Miss whatever-your-name is. So go away—NOW—and leave my soulmate alone!"

****

CATHY

"Grandpa, why was he flirting with that no-name nurse? Is he not happy with just me?" I asked as we left Bill's room.

"He is, and don't you think otherwise. He just can't help himself 'cause he has my flirty gene inside him."

"And what does that mean?" I was bewildered.

"That means he'll always be flamboyant and flirty, but no need to worry because he's just lookin' and teasin'. He loves you as much as I love Grandma, and that's bunches and bunches. Don't you doubt none 'cause he'll never stray."

"I hope you're right, Grandpa, but can I ask you something else? What did

Grandma do when you became flamboyant and flirty with another woman, like Bill was today with that nurse?"

"Easy answer!" he chuckled. She got her broom and thrashed my tail!"

After hesitating, he added, "Of course, I was gonna use another word for tail, yet not in front of a lady. Now let's go watch "Temple Houston" on TV in the waitin' room while Billy sleeps."

****

BILL

I was so exhausted that I fell asleep in a heartbeat. I dreamed of my earlier years on the farm, and goin' to the church youth group. I also dreamed of celebratin' my birthday, and how good it was to wake up each mornin' with the sweet aromas of coffee and Grandma's buttermilk biscuits.

"Billy! It seems that only yesterday you were just bein' born. How quickly time walks away! Happy Birthday, Son," my momma said. As my heart melted like butter in a pan,

I got up thinkin' that later on, after I blew out all eight candles on the cake Grandma made, I would thank God for sendin' me down.

"As I walked over to the window, I looked across the yard at the ol' picket fence and called out, "C'mon, Rooster, it's time to crow! Oh, what's wrong, fella? Did you sleep late this mornin'?" Hmm! Maybe I'll go back to bed and take a short nap too.

Aww, ain't no way I'm goin' back to bed! My stomach's a growlin', and I'm hungry! I hurried to the kitchen table and started slatherin' butter on one of those delicious biscuits. My mouth was a waterin'. I was just about to take a bite when I felt someone tuggin' at my shoulder.

"Hey there, Handsome. We got some good news for you," the nurse said, as she nudged me awake. I opened my eyes and did I get an eyeful! The nurse's large bosom was a bobbin' only inches from my face as she proceeded to shake me. When she saw me starin' in astonishment, she smiled.

"I'm sure glad you're enjoying the sight," she said, again in that sexy sounding voice. "Now, the good news is you've got the okay to leave here tomorrow morning. Doctor's orders. But, I'm going to be so sad to see you go. Tell you what— why don't we tell your girlfriend and Grandpa that visiting hours end early tonight? That way, I can come and read you a bedtime story and tuck you in later. Would you like that?"

I was speechless, but that didn't matter none, because I didn't have a chance to say anythin' even if I was able to. Cathy and Grandpa walked back into the room right then and overheard the nurse's suggestion.

"YOU GET AWAY FROM HIM, YOU HEAR ME?" Cathy screamed as she bolted toward us. In a flash, she was pushin' and clawin' at the nurse, and to my surprise, the nurse was clawin' back. They were havin' a cat fight, right here in the hospital!

"I ain't believin' what I'm a seein'," Grandpa said.

I couldn't believe it either! I pushed the emergency buzzer again, then hollered as best I could above the blarin' alarm, "DOCTOR, DOCTOR, HURRY BEFORE THESE LADIES TEAR EACH OTHER APART!"

"Oh, that doctor better come quickly," Cathy briefly looked at me and hissed. Her eyes were wild with rage, "because when I'm finished with her . . . I'M COMING AFTER YOU!"

CHAPTER 9

~ WHAT IS LOVE ~

CATHY

The nurse's red nails burned like an Indian sunburn as she dug deep into my cheeks, but I continued to fight. Although the emergency alarm had been blaring for a few minutes, the doctor hadn't arrived yet. Grandpa tried once to break us up, but failed.

Bill finally put a halt to things when he extended his arms between our faces and remarked, "Sweet Jesus! Although you're my Angel, you are certainly mean at times, Cathy. Why, the grizzly bears back home would be afraid of you!"

I looked quickly at him, then growled. His comment hurt my feelings. Tears were streaming down my face, mixing with blood from the nurse's wounds.

Grandpa came up from behind me, firmly grabbing both of my shoulders. He spun me around so I was facing the door.

"I'm very disappointed in you, Sweetheart! Now get yourself to the truck. You can see Billy when you come to your senses!"

"Oh Grandpa! You know I love him with all my heart and soul. He needs me," I pleaded.

"Hush! You'd better do as I say!" Letting go of me, he pointed to the exit.

Of course I knew he meant business. I shot the nurse a dirty look, and without saying another word, walked quickly out of the room.

****

Why had I let that nurse get me so angry? After all, I know Bill has Grandpa's flirty and flamboyant genes. When I met him last year, everyone warned me I was in for a heartbreak, but I really think our love is stronger than that. When I saw him eyeing and flirting with her today though, I wanted to die. Maybe the distance between us has changed his feelings for me. After how foolishly I acted, I wouldn't blame him if he told me he wanted to call it quits . . . and if that happens, what will I do? I love him so, and will love him forever and a day, no matter what!

I sat in the truck, crying and cursing myself for letting jealousy get the best of me. I knew I had to get it together, and fast, before I could show my face again.

Since writing has always been therapeutic for me, especially when emotionally upset, I instinctively reached into my handbag for a pen and piece of scrap paper. Wiping the tears from my eyes so I could see, I wrote this poem for Bill.

FOREVER, MY LOVE

Where will your love go
when all's been said and done—
once we've gotten past its newness
with the initial romantic fun?

Will it keep on growing stronger
planting roots for it to stay?
Or will it be forgotten

to wither up, then blow away?

Love Long Distance, it's not easy.
There are times I've worried so
that your love for me may not last,
but Honey, you should know—

there will never be another
who could ever take your place.
Distance, time, or even circumstance
could not divert or begin to erase . . .

all the love I have and hold for you.
It's been strong right from the start—
and it won't go, no, it never will,
because God has sealed it in my heart.

After reading it aloud, I decided to go back into the hospital. I didn't want to end the day without telling Bill I was sorry. I also wanted to give him a goodnight kiss and thank him and Grandpa for putting up with me.

As I walked through the door to his room, he was deep in conversation with another nurse—this one not so pretty. Grandpa was snoozing in a nearby chair.

"Geez! Where have you been, Angel?" Bill said when he saw me.

"Grandpa sent me out to the truck to calm down, remember?" My face turned a little red. I was still ashamed at how badly I had acted.

"What's going on?" I asked him. "Is everything okay?"

"This is Marsha. She's my new nurse, Darlin'. The other nurse has been fired."

Marsha looked at me and smiled. I already liked her a whole lot better. "We're waiting on his test results from the lab," she interjected. "They'll be ready in 30 minutes. If all looks good, Bill will be heading back with you and his grandpa to Tennessee for a little rest and relaxation before he goes back into training."

Grandpa woke up and heard this. "Billy! I almost forgot!" he exclaimed. "I brought along your writin' from way back yonder when you was just a junior 'towhead'. Quite frankly, you were also a pain in my 'you-know-what' at times! I can sure remember when you won that school writin' contest. You were about 14 then if my memory's correct."

"That's right, you ain't lost it yet," Bill replied.

Grandpa rubbed his eyes, got up out of the chair and stretched before adding, "Anyways, I thought you'd enjoy readin' them stories you wrote, but now that you may be leavin' the hospital already . . . "

Bill interrupted. "Aww, that's okay, Grandpa! Thank you for your kindness, and I'll tell ya what—I can read some of those stories to Cathy as we bump along the road to home."

"It's gonna be crowded inside that truck, Billy. I didn't know you'd be comin' home with us."

"No problem!" Bill quickly responded. "We'll just get us some hay for the truckbed. Cathy and I can ride in the back. *Goody, Goody*!"

****

BILL

It was a gorgeous day as we drove away from the hospital. Grandpa had found hay at a nearby farm, and we were headed for the Smoky Mountains. Snuggled up close to each other, Cathy and I sang 'happy songs' as Grandpa drove the ol' truck along.

After sharin' a cold Pop-Tart with Cathy, and washin' it down with TAB soda, I started readin' her one of my stories from the writin' composition book that Grandpa had brought me.

"Are you listenin', Darlin'? Here goes . . . ."

Written by Billy (age 14)
WHAT IS LOVE?

I was eight years old, hidin' behind a door in our little log cabin one night, hearin' Grandpa whisperin' words of love to Grandma while they were lyin' in their bed.

"Aww, Honey! Have you ever given any thought as to what love is?" Grandpa asked.

"Hmm . . . not really, but I'll bet you're gonna tell me," Grandma replied.

"You know me well," he said, "so you know I think about these philosophical things from time to time. To me, love is livin', givin', and unselfishly sharin' with one another, the beautiful creations of God while walkin' along the pathway to happiness."

Grandpa cleared his throat and turned the light off. Then he kept on talkin'.

"My father once told me, and I agree, that love is also God's way of wakin' us from the sad dreams of yesterday, wipin' the tears from our eyes, and teachin' us happy songs for our tomorrows."

"You have always been so poetic," Grandma said.

"Well I try to be," Grandpa replied.

"After that, he mentioned me, and my ears really perked up."

"Do you remember tellin' me after Billy was born that love is like watchin' a mother smile while holdin' her child, then kissin' away its cries? And it's like hearin' her say I love you, then thankin' God for His gift? Do you remember that, Sweetheart —do you, huh?"

"Oh I remember, Handsome, but now you're gettin' carried away! C'mon, count yourself some sheep, and let's get some sleep before the rooster crows."

****

CATHY

"*Brrr!* Stop hoggin' all the hay and roll over this way, 'cause there's a chill in the air!" Bill was teasing me. I knew he wanted to snuggle up closer so he could . . . better not say!

"I'm headed on over there, Honey, and I'm so very hot for you. I'll keep you warm, all right!" I replied, knowing that would get him going.

"Light my fire, Baby, Baby! Oh, yes, *YESSS!*"

He was full of expectation, and it was making me blush, but then I got distracted by a nearby sight and exclaimed, "My goodness! Just look over there at those little baby ducks. Aren't they cute? See them waddle behind their mama along the pond as she fights off them hungry crows hovering above her head?"

"You betcha I see them! Once again, it reminds me of Grandpa's words tellin' Grandma what love is. Now come on over here, and I'll tell ya the rest."

Bill pulled me closer to him. After kissing me deeply, he said, "Grandpa also told me that love is like seein' baby deer feedin' nearby, and slowly fallin' rain; awakin' from a dream of fishin' in a stream and catchin' Speckled Mountain Trout."

"It's seeing the autumn leaves fall from the trees, spiral in the breeze, then walk along the ground as little squirrels scamper for nuts," I added.

"And lastly, yet above all the others, it's sharin' hugs and lovin' one another," we both recited together.

"I remember you telling me that part, exactly like that, under the willow tree," I said.

Bill gave me another kiss, this one much longer, then smiled and replied, "I believe that's what love is, Darlin'!"

"I believe it too, Honey! I really do. I, as well. . ." The truck suddenly swayed a bit. I glanced over at the rear window and met Grandpa's eyes. "Honey, why's Grandpa looking at us when he should be watching where he's going?"

The truck swayed again, this time wider. We saw Grandpa grab his flask to sneak himself a sip of moonshine.

"Made special by a young fella in the Smoky Mountains named "Popcorn" Sutton, I'll bet," Bill remarked. "He's just calmin' his nerves some. It'll be alright."

Then Grandpa started fiddling with the radio. He turned up the volume when he came to a song that was playing—"There I've Said it Again" by Bobby Vinton.

"Now he's humming along to the song and settling down," I added. His steering was back on track, and I tried to relax— maybe Bill was right.

"I'll bet he's reminiscin' back to when he and Grandma used to sneak in the barn to make out in the hay, before they were married," Bill remarked. "Look, he's smokin' up the glass with his nose. That reminds me—Grandma told me once that Grandpa's nose is always cold when he kisses her."

I would've laughed at the comment, but the truck began swerving this way and that again; the tires started squealing.

"Aren't you worried about the way he's driving?" I shrieked. "He's gonna get us . . ."

Grandpa slammed on the brakes and there was a loud crash.

"OH MY GOD—HELP US!" I screamed.

CHAPTER 10

~ THE WILLOW TREE ~

BILL

Lightnin' flashed; thunder roared. A violent wind blew across Grandpa's ol' truck, accompanied by a drenchin' rain. It became crystal clear that God had heard Cathy scream. Chickens squawked all around us as they flapped their wings, then we saw feathers fill the air. If I hadn't been holdin' her tightly, she might've been thrown from the truck and possibly killed.

Grandpa began to jibber-jabber words of obscenity, and despite the rain, quickly opened the truck door, stumblin' onto the ground. Wobblin' like a duck, he headed toward the driver of the chicken truck. We could see his hands were tightly clenched and ready for battle.

"Lord Almighty! What's a matta' with you, Mister? Stoppin' that abruptly in front of me caused all of this to happen. So, before you go off to jail, I'm gonna whup your tail!"

"Please don't! I'm not a 'Mister'—I'm a lady."

He wiped the water from his glasses so he could see. His attitude changed in a heartbeat. Rather than continuin' to rant and rave, he smiled, winked, and blew her a kiss before replyin', "A beautiful one too! What is your name, Sweetheart?"

"You may call me Bunny, Honey!" she cooed, winkin' back at him.

"Shame on both of you! I saw what you just did, Grandpa. Although she's a pretty thing in those bib overalls with her hair pinned up, you are married to Grandma," I said as I walked up to them.

"Aw, I'm so sorry! There are times I can't control my flirty ways. It's all my fault," the lady confessed. "Let me officially introduce myself. My name is Elizabeth, and I'm a cheerleader for the Alabama Crimson Tide football team. Ever heard of 'em?"

"Yes, I have," Grandpa replied. "They got Joe Namath as their quarterback. Very fine team and a good coach, too. Billy, remember me tellin' you the story about Bear Bryant?"

I had to chuckle. "Sure do! He wrestled with a bear when he was only 13."

"Well, I'm surprised to hear that," Elizabeth exclaimed. "Now please forgive me for stalling in front of you. I don't know how to drive a shift so well. My boyfriend's gonna have my hide for causin' an accident and losin' his precious chickens."

"Aww Honey, there's really no damage. Only thing is the chicken crates slid and crashed onto the front of my truck—they all busted out of jail. I'll help find 'em if you'd like. You'll help, won't ya, Billy?"

"I don't think I've got any choice now, do I?"

****

CATHY

After searching here and there, Bill and Grandpa had gathered up all the chickens and returned to the truck. We were soon on our way again. Even though it was still raining, we put Grandpa in back on the hay so he could sober up. No more moonshine or mishaps along the way.

I insisted on driving, so Bill sat next to me. As we rode along, I could see him looking at my legs, then he slowly put his hand on my knee.

"Behave!" I demanded. "I have to concentrate and you're making it awfully hard. Now rest while you can." I put my hand in his and he gave it a squeeze before reluctantly resting his back by his side.

"Honey, get some sleep," I said. Tonight you can recite words of poetry to me under the willow tree, and afterwards we can . . . you know! Does that sound like a good plan?"

"Yes, Ma'am!" Bill replied. "It's a date; I can't wait!"

****

It was pitch dark when I pulled into the dirt driveway of the log cabin Bill had grown up in. His momma and grandma had spent all day preparing for our arrival. The aromas of country fried chicken, mashed potatoes with gravy, and buttermilk biscuits filled the air and danced under our noses as we walked in.

"Oh my God! I'm so hungry! There's nothin' better than your cookin', Grandma." Bill exclaimed.

Grandma dabbed her eyes with the edge of her apron to wipe away the tears of happiness she was shedding. "It's nice to see you back—I've missed ya, Billy!"

Bill hugged his momma next, and said, "Sorry I was gone so long, but I'm home now for a bit. I love you, Momma."

"You hush on up, my son, or you'll get me cryin' too. Now, let's everyone hurry and eat before it gets cold," she replied.

Grandpa, Bill and I didn't need convincing. We all quickly found our places at the table. As he always did, Grandpa started with a blessing.

"Heavenly Father! Unselfishly I ask, please reach down Your hand and destroy the jugs of moonshine I have buried all around. Then change me from this creature I am. The Bible tells us many things. Some are at the forefront of our priorities. Tonight, I humble myself before You, knowin' that there are those who don't have a roof over their heads and are disabled. You ask us to care for our fellow man and woman, yet sometimes I tend to forget about them. I do believe in You and ask that my grandson, Billy, follow You along the pathway of tomorrow and find the special purpose in his life. Let him be what others need, Lord. This is all I ask. In Your Holy Name, Amen."

****

After we were all done eating, I cleared the table and washed the dishes. Bill came up behind me and whispered, "C'mon Beautiful, let me take you down to the willow tree where we'll listen to the whippoorwills courting. The owls will hoot and the coyotes howl while we make our own music under the beautiful sky—oh yes!"

Hand-in-hand we walked through the meadow, under the stars and a silver moon above, professing our love and thanks for being together. When we reached the willow tree, Bill spread a blanket underneath it, and as we lay side-by-side, he recited poetry before we fell asleep to the sound of a whippoorwill calling for its mate. We didn't sleep for long because we still had lots of kissing to do.

"My heart belongs to you forever," he said with his arms wrapped around me. "My life holds so many gifts and you're the greatest one. I'll never stop lovin' you."

"Do you promise?" I asked him.

"Cross my heart and hope to die." Now, c'mon Baby, give me some sugar."

"I'll bite your tongue, that's what I'll do! I can feel you patting my tail," I replied. "Oh my, you're already getting frisky!"

"What do ya mean, pattin' your tail? My hands aren't there . . . they're higher."

That's when I saw it. "Bill! There's a big panther peeking through the branches; it's about to pounce on us!"

CHAPTER 11

~ A SALUTE TO GRANDPA

~

CATHY

Bill immediately started to chuckle. "That's no panther, Darlin', it's just Grandpa," he said.

"My heart's done skipped a hundred beats!" I exclaimed. "What are you doing sneaking up on us that way, Grandpa? You scared the living daylights out of me."

"Why of course I did; that's what I intended to do. Did you also feel me pokin' your behind with a stick? I know you have a wild imaginative mind, but I didn't mean to scare ya that much. It must've been my shiny teeth that did it." Grandpa put a flashlight up to the side of his cheek, opened his mouth, baring his full set of dentures, then turned the flashlight on. "See? Now I can understand how you thought this here mouth belonged to a panther. Truth be told, though, many don't believe they exist in the Smoky Mountains. However, I'm here to tell ya they do, 'cause I've seen them with my own two eyes!"

"Okay Grandpa, you can tell us that story later. Now, can't you see we want to be alone? What's all this about? It's not Halloween, so it can't be trick or treat," Bill replied.

Grandpa found his way through the branches to come and sit down beside us.

"Shee! I know you two want to be alone, but I also feel that both of you need to know what may or may not happen here tonight. Therefore, I need to share a certain story with both of ya. So, take an intermission and listen up!"

"Okay, but it better be a short intermission 'cause I've got miles to go before I sleep again," Bill remarked.

"Of course both of you know I'm a full-blooded Indian," Grandpa began. "Back when I was a few years younger than Billy,

I became a US citizen and met Grandma. However, our datin' wasn't accepted since she was Irish and had no Indian blood. So we secretly began our romance, fell in love, then night after night, we met under this same willow tree."

Bill looked over at me, flirtingly winked his eye, and blew me a kiss. He had an idea what Grandpa was going to say next.

"A few months later, Grandma's family found out about us. Her daddy forbade us to see each other and said no preacher would ever marry us. Grandma thought it was hopeless that we'd ever wed. Her tears were flowin' like a river that night when she told me about it. We were right here on a blanket, like the two of you. Well I was hearin' none of it! I told her we'd marry anyway."

Bill and I were now totally entranced by his story, although we had no idea how it pertained to us. It didn't take long to find out though, because Grandpa wasn't finished yet.

"We said our vows together that same night, then I made love to her. It was the best night of our lives, and one we both still talk about. A couple years later, we were allowed to get "officially" married in the chapel, although in our hearts we were committed and married long before that. Do I think God is angry at us for what we did? No way!"

Grandpa looked directly into my eyes and continued.

"Billy is headed back soon and there's no tellin' what will happen next. You know what I mean; we almost lost him already. So without sayin' any more, I want to tell you to listen to and follow your heart! Not just to the excitement stirrin' in both of you, but really listen. God will speak to you there and tell you if it's wrong or if it's right. Long story short, I hope you take my advice."

Getting himself up from the blanket, Grandpa crawled out from under the tree and walked away. Once we could hear his footsteps no longer, Bill cuddled up to me again, then said in his charming manner, "I believe you were about to bite my tongue before Grandpa came along."

I was already listening to what God was telling me. "Honey, we gave our vows to each other before when you left for training, remember?"

"Of course I remember, Beautiful. And I meant every word I said in those vows. Be it now and always, "I love you heart and soul, Cathy."

"And I love you even more than that, my Mountain Man. I'll be yours forever and a day."

Pressing up closer to Bill, I gave him that little love bite before whispering in his ear, "It's time that we consummate this marriage, like Grandpa and Grandma did."

"Hurrah!" Bill exclaimed, needing no convincing. He then made love to me, slowly and gently, under the willow tree. We were now no longer two, but one, and in my heart, I recalled Matthew 19:6 from the Bible—"*What God has joined together, let no man put asunder*"—so I knew we'd never part.

Afterward, while we were relaxing, we could see the full moon peeking through and shining down on us. We talked about a science fiction novel we both had recently read—"Cat's Cradle" by Kurt Vonnegut.

Bill fell asleep first, while we were still wrapped in each other's arms. A gentle wind blew across the meadow as I recalled another Bible verse—"*Go my children, be fruitful and multiply, fill the earth, then subdue it; rule over the fish of the sea and the birds of the air, then over every creature that walks or crawls upon the earth."* (Genesis 1:28)

A lone wolf was now the one crying for its mate, but I heard no answer. "Aww, it's okay, fella," I repeated the words I'd heard Bill say before, "'cause your girlfriend probably has a headache tonight."

I smiled as I closed my eyes. In no time, I was fast asleep too, and neither of us awoke again until the morning sun warmed our faces.

****

I didn't want to let Bill go as we said our goodbyes at the train station. To know that when he finished training, he would be headed to Vietnam, subject to injury or possibly killed in the awful war, seemed unbearable.

Bill held me close, kissed me, then whispered, "What we shared last night will give me comfort through the days ahead, and I'll give it my best shot to return to you, Beautiful. But now I have to serve God and country. Should anythin' happen to me, just remember, God has blessed us with a union that will last forever. I love you more than the breath that's in me."

We were still kissing when the train whistle blew, signaling it was time for him to leave. I let go of him, reluctantly, as salty tears ran down my face. The train pulled away moments later. It was love long distance once again.

I then fell down on my knees, locked my hands together, looked toward Heaven, and asked God, *"Will I see him come back? Please keep my soulmate safe and bring him back home to me!"*

CHAPTER 12

~ THE GREATEST GIFT ~

April 24, 1964

Dear Diary,

The loneliness I've been feeling since Bill went back to training has been unbearable, especially at night. I go to bed early, eager to dream of us under the willow tree, making sweet, passionate love. I can feel his big strong hands on my skin, his warm breath in my hair, his muscular body pressed against mine, igniting such a burning desire—a fire—within me. I can hear him whisper, "I love you" in my ear, taste his deep and delicious kisses, and when he starts to explore . . . oh, I can't write any more because I'm afraid someone else might read this!

As I experienced the stabbing pain of lost innocence that first night, I think about how Bill was so gentle and understanding. The unbounded pleasures came flooding in, washing the pain away, as we united in love, under God, with the big bright stars shining through the willow tree branches. "They're winking at you," Bill had said. I told him they were just giving their approval.

The hard part about having been granted the joy of seeing Bill again, so soon and unexpectedly, was the heartbreak of having to say goodbye to him once more. I feel so alone and incomplete without him and cry endlessly. It feels like I've fallen into a deep, dark well and am unable to get out. Why does it have to be like this? Still, I am thankful that his Grandpa and Grandma have taken me in, allowing me to stay with them until his return.

Love Long Distance

****

April 28, 1964

Hi Honey,

I ran to the mailbox today, right after getting home from a short trip with Grandpa, hoping to find a letter from you. There wasn't one. I know you told me you would write as soon as you could, but I can't wait any longer. It's been a week since you left, and I miss you so much!

Guess what? Grandpa took me to Nashville! He said it was my early birthday gift. First stop, of course, was 116 Fifth Avenue North — home of the Grand Ole Opry. No performance, but he wanted me to see it. Now when we listen to their show on the radio on Saturday nights, I'll be able to picture it in my mind. He explained that they originally opened on the fifth floor radio station studio of the National Life & Accident Insurance Company in downtown Nashville on November 28, 1925. They called it the "WSM Barn Dance" back then. That was the day he turned 27, and he, along with Grandma, listened to the 77-year-old fiddler, Uncle Jimmy Thompson, on their radio show that night.

Afterwards we had a picnic lunch on a bench at Nashville's first "instant park," located in the burnt-out cavity of the former Maxwell House site. We then went to the Pepsi Open House at Beamon Bottling Company on Thompson Lane. There were tons of people gathered outside, and one excited woman told me why. Joan Crawford was there! Although it was a long wait in line, I was thrilled to finally meet her and get her autograph.

Next we visited Nashville's Municipal Auditorium where there was another big crowd. Oral Roberts was the attraction, and he was on stage preaching about talking in tongues and the perils of sin. When he asked people to come join him to be saved, many did—including me. Grandpa sure was proud. He was grinning from ear-to-ear when I got back from being prayed over. He told me he'd been saved several years ago, and so had you. Later on I asked him if tongues was like "Smoky Mountain" talk, and he said it was jibber-jabber all right, but of a different kind.

I thought we'd be heading home after that, but Grandpa was too tired to drive back, so we stayed overnight at the Holiday Inn on West End Avenue. The next morning, there were Civil Rights protesters sitting in the street. Grandpa said we'd best get on our way before things started heating up.

Oh my, I've written so much! I do hope to hear from you soon. Please let me know how things are going there and if you are all right. I pray to God every day and night for your safety.

"HKAYK!"

All My Love,

Cathy

P.S. Now that I know when Grandpa's birthday is, I'm going to make sure we have a grand celebration for him. I don't know if they'll allow you another short leave, but if possible, the best gift he could ever receive is you. He loves you heart and soul, like I do. Of course I want to see you too, and we could make love a few more times. Oh YESSS! It may be too cold in November to romance under our willow tree, but that's all right—we'll move our lovemaking to the hay loft in the barn instead! Wouldn't that be fun? I can remember us sneaking up there last Halloween night after you gave an entertaining fright to those little kids who came to the door. While you held me in your arms so tight, you asked me if I wanted a trick or a treat. When I said treat, you showered me with dozens of sweet, sweet kisses and love bites. We started making out, and it was getting hot and heavy. That's when some troublemaking teenagers snuck into the barn and were drinking moonshine. When they saw you jump down from the hay loft, they ran out of there! You must've chased after them for a good fifteen minutes, remember? Oh, it seems like it was so long ago! Who would've thought we'd soon be apart?

P.P.S. Please ignore any tear stains you may find on this letter. I'm crying now, so I'm going to close my eyes and meet you in my dreams tonight.

****

May 7, 1964

My Darlin',

Happy Birthday, Baby! I just received the letter you wrote on April 28th. How sweet of Grandpa to take you to Nashville! Please forgive me for the late response. I've been so busy with training since I got back here.

I do hope you received the dozen long-stemmed red roses I sent you as a birthday gift. See? I didn't forget! The florist manager assured me they would arrive on time. Oh how I wish I were with you to celebrate, and even though you'll get this letter a little late, I want to say that thinkin' back on our life, we've had our share of good times. We've seen some tough times, too—days when just knowin' we had each other made all the difference. I know that as long as you're beside me, I have everythin' I need to be happy. I love bein' in love with an angel like you. I love that you're strong enough to be gentle, brave enough to be carin', and sensitive enough to know how to make me feel really loved. To me, that's the ultimate measure of a woman. I'm so lucky to have you in my life.

I shall never forget the intimacy we shared before I left for commando training. It was a magnificent evenin' in the meadow back home. The moon was full as we sat under the willow tree listenin' to a whippoorwill call for its mate.

You were flauntin' it big time, Beautiful! You sashayed this way and that, did a seductive twist of your hips, crooked your finger at me, then blew me a kiss. After Grandpa came and told us his *story, we cuddled up next to one another on the blanket, made love for the first time, then fell asleep. I dreamed of you all dressed in a gorgeous blue nightgown, and I could see the matchin' lace lingerie. Shee!*

Yes, Darlin', I dreamed of our yesterday in the meadow, and how you are the happiness I cherish and my dearest friend. You are my soulmate and confidante; you are everythin' to me. You are all the true things in life: family, laughter, and love. You're what makes my heart dance, and my world shine. I'm forever changed by your love and so grateful; I just want to again say, "I love you!" The greatest gift of all is the two of us together forever.

Beginnin' tomorrow night, I'll be doin' three additional hours of "hand-to-hand" martial arts training to make up for the time lost when hospitalized. Of course I know Grandpa's birthday is in November. However, I'll not be comin' home again 'cause I'll already be in Vietnam. Therefore, always remember that when your nights are lonely, and bed is bare,

just touch my picture...and I'll be there."
You betcha! "HKAYK!" Later . . .

All my Love,

Bill

CHAPTER 13

~ JOINED AT THE HIP ~

May 10, 1964

My Dearest Darlin',

Today is Sunday, and I have a few minutes for writin'. I'm listenin' to "Hello, Dolly" by Louis Armstrong, thinkin' of our first date, those to follow . . . and now feelin' as though half of my heart is missin'. To me, happiness is bein' with you. I live with the memory of your caresses and affectionate solicitude. The sweet fragrance of your body continually burns and glows like a flame in my heart. As soulmates, we should feel the freedom to express our needs and our hurts, seven days a week, 24 hours a day.

Fightin' for our love and never considerin' bein' apart, other than for the call of freedom, should forever be our goal in life.

Growin' with one another into the autumn of our lives, walkin' hand-in-hand and joined at the hip, down the pathway to happiness is what I live for. Our bein' together is simply a present from The Almighty, and I thank Him for the gift. I want you to know that when God made you, He threw away the mold, said "I'm pleased," then sent you down to me. I needed you then, I need you now . . . and I'll need you through all of our tomorrows. And through it all, I pledge to stand tall and be true to you. Please try to understand that I'm just a man, must complete my training here, and then go to Vietnam. Of course, there's no doubt I'll forge the fires in the pits of hell. At times I'll stumble, fall, bleed; yet, Ol' Glory shall wave forever. Should God call me home while servin' my country and fightin' for its honor, my spirit will be with you always.

I've got to go now, Beautiful. I hope you realize how very much I love and miss you.

I'll write again later—God willin'.

"HKAYK!"

All My Love Forever,

Bill

****

May 14, 1964

Dear Diary,

The trip to Nashville was great, and being saved was life changing. For days after that very emotional experience, I was on cloud 9. The sky was brighter; the grass greener. All I wanted to do was talk about it.

On my birthday, I received a dozen red roses from Bill. It was a nice surprise, and they are still so beautiful. It made my heart sing to know he was thinking of me. I kept hoping the phone would ring—that he'd be able to call—but it didn't happen.

After that, though, my mood began to change. An overwhelming sadness has crept up on me once again, wrapping itself around me. I call it the devil himself trying to squeeze the life out of me. The world appears not so bright and new anymore. Rather, it seems dark and gray. I can't seem to get out of my own way. I'm shaking inside—tremors of anxiety. Sleep is my only comfort; food doesn't interest me. All I do is cry when I'm awake. I'm worried that I'm going through some sort of depression. Why did God allow this to happen after being saved? And what if something bad happens to Bill while he's away? God forbid, but my mind races with thoughts of doom and gloom. I try to tell it to shut up. I pray for help—for the light to turn back on and get me through this deep, dark dungeon I find myself in—but for some reason, God has let Satan take over and have his way. Is this a test of my faith? Like Job? I pray, unceasingly, for answers.

****

Love Long Distance

May 15, 1964

My Darlin',

Today is Friday and it is 9 pm. We're through with training until Monday, 5 am. You should've received my letter of May 10th by now. I haven't heard from you since April 28th, and I hope nothin's wrong. Back on March 7th, I told you I'd be goin, to the Naval Explosive Ordnance School for 16 weeks, then a Joint Services Commando School for 19 weeks. I was notified today that the total weeks of training would be 37, rather than 35. Of course that don't stop babies from cryin' and dogs from barkin'. I'm just keepin' you on the same page with me.

I'm relaxin' on the cot now and missin' you like a baby deer misses its momma who was shot and killed by a farmer for his family's supper. I remember, so very well, the year I turned 12, and Grandpa took me deer huntin' in the north woods. The sun was risin' above the trees as we headed out through the high grass in the meadow. I walked along, filled with pride, carryin' Grandpa's shotgun on my shoulder, just like Davy Crockett.

Just then, we came to an old trail leadin' into the woods. The birds were already singin' their hellos, and the lone wolf was on his way home from who knows where. Quickly raisin' his hand, Grandpa stopped short.

"Quiet, Billy! Do you see the deer under the cedar tree?"

"Oh, I see it, Grandpa. But it looks so small and all. I just betcha it slipped away from its momma, then got lost."

"Don't you remember my tellin' you, 'a bird in hand is better than two in a bush'? Now get the shotgun off your shoulder, shoot the critter, and we'll have venison steak for supper."

"I know I'll not be your hero now, Grandpa, 'cause I can't shoot the baby deer and leave its momma to wander, here and yonder, tryin' to find it. I remember, as well, you tellin' me that God said, 'show kindness to My earthly creatures, and My door shall be open to you.'"

"Okay Billy! We'll not have venison steak for supper, but rather, leftovers from last night. It's alright, too, because you'll be my hero forevermore . . . and that's for sure!"

Shee! I know you like me sharin' these true stories Grandpa saved. I'm so tired and sleepy now, Darlin', yet I just had to send my heart to you on a golden platter while sayin' goodnight. I'll dream of you, hold you tight, then whisper, "I love you more today than I did yesterday, and I'll love you more tomorrow." I need you like fish need water, Beautiful. Please write to me soon! God Bless.

All My Love Forever,

XOX

Bill

******

May 15, 1964

Hello Billy,

Before I go on, I want to assure you that Cathy will be okay, so please don't worry. She is in good hands at the Tennessee Psychiatric Hospital and Institute in Memphis. It's kind of a far piece down the road, but it's only for a short time, and we've been told that it's the best place for her.

Grandma and I have been concerned about her. She was very depressed after you left here, so that's why I took her to Nashville. It was wonderful to see her smilin' again. And then when she was saved, why, I was thrilled to witness that! She cried buckets of happy tears that day. Once we got back home, we marveled at her improved state of mind.

Unfortunately, things have since changed, though. She's stopped eatin' and is constantly sleepin'. We are worried once more. The final straw came yesterday when she didn't even come out of her room. When I asked her what was wrong, she wouldn't respond. At Grandma's insistence, I had to reach out and get her some help. Oh, what that poor girl is goin' through!

Love Long Distance

The doctor there guarantees us she'll be alright. He wants to keep her in the hospital for observation, but she'll be comin' home again soon. He assures us that rest and relaxation, along with some therapy, is what she needs right now.

Your letter to her came today, and we will bring it to her when we visit. I'm sure it will cheer her up. Again, please don't worry. Cathy has been prayin', and both Grandma and I have been prayin' too. It's traumatic for her to be away from you, and, as you know, she is a sensitive soul. I keep wonderin' why God is lettin' her go through this. Grandma says God has His reasons.

Grandma and your mama send their love, along with mine. Of course you know that Cathy loves you so very much too. I'm sure you'll also be receivin' a letter from her soon. My brave young man, we are all so proud of you!

Respectfully,

Grandpa

CHAPTER 14

~ CRAZY OVER YOU ~

CATHY

Tossing and turning in my sleep, I screamed, *"Dear God! Why have You forsaken me by sending Bill so far away? Can't you see my heart is breaking? Can't you see the sad tears in my eyes? Please, please . . . help me find peace of mind."*

Around midnight I awoke in a strange room to the sound of shuffling in the hallway. Someone was being transported, unwillingly, into the hospital.

"Those monsters are coming after me!" a woman screamed.

I felt so sad for her, and I thought, "There but for the grace of God, go I."

"Oh, no! Please don't lock me up. Someone help me," she cried.

"STAT! Put her in the straight-jacket," an orderly called.

She kept screaming and pleading. My heart went out to her. It reminded me of the book "One Flew Over the Cuckoo's Nest" by Ken Kesey.

"She must be schizophrenic," I thought. Will they give her shock therapy? Or maybe a lobotomy? The thought ran shivers up my spine as I crept to the door to take a quick look at her.

What was I doing here? My situation was quite different since I had admitted myself voluntarily. Wiping my eyes, I apologized to God for my impatience. Then I prayed hard for all those less fortunate.

Before daybreak, when all seemed calm again, I quietly got out of bed and walked down to the "padded room" which is for high-risk patients to prevent them from hurting themselves. The door was locked, but had a small shatterproof observation window. After checking to make sure no one was watching, I put my eyes up to it and peeked in. The woman who was screaming last night was huddled in the corner with her eyes closed. I could hear her singing, although very softly, a familiar and beautiful song. The words reached out and touched my soul.

"Amazing Grace, how sweet the sound, that saved a wretch like me..."

****

GRANDPA

It was the middle of the night when the phone rang. I hurried to the kitchen to answer it. I didn't even have a chance to say hello.

""What's goin' on there! I just got the letter tellin' me Cathy's in the hospital!"

"Billy, calm down now! She's gonna be fine. Why are you callin' me at this hour?"

"How can I help, Grandpa? I had to call right away 'cause I'm worried sick! Should I try for an emergency leave through the Red Cross?"

"There's nothin' you can do. As I said, she's gonna be fine!"

"Did the doctor medicate her, and is she still depressed? Why was she in the friggin' hospital in the first place?"

"Questions, questions! Take a deep breath, hush up, and listen for a change. You never were good at that!"

"Mind your manners, Grandpa . . . and don't yell at me. I'm worried!"

"I'm sorry, Billy. Cathy has been very depressed. Grandma and I were beside ourselves seein' her that way. As you know, she's usually so positive and upbeat. We had to get some help. The doctor suggested runnin' some tests because Cathy has depression in her family. Her great uncle was manic-depressive and died in an alley from self-inflicted starvation. They needed to find out if her depression was hereditary. Also, they didn't wanna guess whether or not she was suicidal. Since the hospital is more than a hop, skip and jump away, it was suggested she stay for a few days."

"Okay, I understand. When will she be goin' home? She's not crazy, is she?"

"Oh, she's crazy all right—crazy over you! Cathy's made herself sick thinkin' about your welfare and what might happen when you go to 'Nam. She's lost her ability to reason. It's been quite a struggle; yet she's not suicidal. I could've told ya that right from the get-go."

"Are they givin' her Valium? "

"No, no meds, Billy. Instead, the doctor suggested meditation to relax and ease her mind over time."

"Thanks for the better news. Now, tell me how to reach Cathy 'cause I want to tell her again that I love her heart and soul."

****

CATHY

We were all waiting for our morning stretches and group therapy. "Hey, want a cigarette?" The woman who had been in the padded room extended a Viceroy to me.

"No, thank you," I replied. "The Surgeon General says cigarette smoking is dangerous."

She put the cigarette back into the pack before she sat down next to me and sarcastically responded, "La-di-da, Goody-Two-Shoes!" Periodically blowing smoke rings, she continued to stare at me with glazed eyes. I could tell she was heavily medicated.

The radio was on, and the song playing was "Crazy" by Patsy Cline. A guy sitting across from us started laughing hysterically. He exclaimed, "I'm crazy, you're crazy, we're all crazy, crazy!"

I was about to say, 'I am not,' but that's when the nurse on duty walked into the room.

"Cathy, you have a phone call," the nurse announced.

"It must be Grandma or Grandpa." I stood up to follow her. "Tomorrow they're coming to get me." I had to admit I was glad to be getting out of this place.

"Hello," I said into the mouthpiece.

"Hey Beautiful! I love you! And always remember how much. Please get better for me, okay?"

"Honey! I've missed you terribly, and I love you more than you love me!"

My heart seemed to go pitter-patter, skipping a beat. I was so happy to hear Bill's voice. We talked for over an hour, and when I closed my eyes that night, I drifted into an awesome dream of the two of us making love under the willow tree.

****

The doctor came to see me the next morning.

"Thank you, Doctor, for all you've done. I truly feel the time here has helped."

"I've already seen an improvement, Cathy. Based on these observations, along with the results of several tests, there's no need to prescribe any medications at this time. However, once you get back home, if your depressive state gets worse instead of better, call immediately. Do you understand?"

"Yes, I promise. Now please keep everything we've discussed between us."

"Of course! Patient confidentiality is very important in my professional practice of psychiatry. I can't share anything, nor would I, without your approval and written permission."

****

Such a long journey home, but it was nice talking with Grandpa along the way. Grandma wasn't with us. Instead, she was preparing to welcome us with a delicious supper. I was glad to get back to the little log cabin, but, oh, how I miss Bill!

****

Love Long Distance

It was pitch dark as I sat alone on the blanket beneath the willow tree that night. Grandpa wasn't far away, making sure I was all right, but the only things in my sight were the lights of a thousand fireflies. "What a blessing to behold," I whispered to myself.

"Are you gonna join me, Bill?" I said inside my head. Just then, the wind rustled through the leaves of the trees, and seemed to whisper, *"I'm with you in spirit, Beautiful. And by the grace of God, we'll never part."*

"Are You listening, God? Please, remember to bring Bill safely home to me; I cant live without him!"

I began wondering what our future would hold. After a little while, I started getting tired and sleepy. As I quickly stood up and started folding the blanket, a wave of dizziness overtook me and I almost fell. I became nauseated, and that startled me. "Oh my God! Could it be true? Could I possibly be...?"

CHAPTER 15

~ HURRAH, COMMANDO! ~

CATHY

"It's so great that Bill's been able to call a few times a week," I commented to Grandma and Grandpa. "I sure wish he were coming with us."

"May God protect him while he's away," Grandma replied. "Lord willin', he'll be travelin' these roads many times again, as he did when he was just a little boy. He's always loved the Smoky Mountains. Why, I remember him sayin' he'd like his ashes spread throughout these mountains if'n..."

"Grandma, hush on up!" interrupted Grandpa. "We're gonna be lookin' down from Heaven a long, long time before that ever happens!" He glanced back at me through his rearview mirror and said, "Billy's gonna come on home safe and sound. Knowin' how strong and brave that boy is, I'm sure he'll be covered in medals of honor too."

Grandpa was driving the truck and concentrating on the road. He was also focused on the flask of moonshine hidden in the inside pocket of his coat. Grandma would whoop him with her broom, real hard, if she found out. Taking even a sip right now was out of the question.

As we drove through the Smoky Mountains, heading east, the 42 miles to Cherokee, North Carolina, seemed extra-long today. Once they arrived there, where Uncle Luke (Luga, in Indian) lived, Grandpa planned to make a quick getaway with his brother so they could drink that moonshine.

"So, what did Billy have to say when he called this mornin'?" Grandma asked.

"I'll spare you the mushy stuff, which was about 90 percent of our conversation. Actually, would you mind much if I told you later. My stomach's a little queasy all of a sudden. In fact, it's a lot queasy! Grandpa, stop the truck...NOW!"

Grandpa quickly pulled off to the side of the road, and I got out just in time. Lurching forward, I lost the contents of my stomach in a matter of seconds. When I sat back down in my seat and closed the passenger door, I apologized for getting sick. That's when Grandpa handed me a folded up map.

"I wish I had some mint leaves with me, but I ain't wearin' my bib overalls, and that's where I keep 'em. Here, open this map up some and press it against your belly, young lady. It also helps car sickness. My, my, this here's the second time you've gone and done this on me."

"But, Grandpa...."

"No buts! Listen up, because I know what I'm talkin' about." He looked at me sternly until I did as he said.

Grandma was quick to put in her two cents. "You've been rather peaked lately. Maybe you're comin' down with somethin'."

"No, I'll be okay. No worries." But I was worried. What if . . . The time was moving on, and I'd find out soon enough.

We continued along on our journey, and although I figured the reservation itself would be quite interesting, and I was eager to meet another member of Bill's family, it was the cherry picking I was most looking forward to. Grandma told me it was prime picking time there, and North Carolina had the best black cherries around. We were going to get us enough to bake a couple of pies when we got back home again. One would be for Grandpa, and the other one I'd ship to Bill. Oh, he'll be thrilled because he sure does love cherry pie!

Before we did get back home though, we'd return by way of Nashville to finally see a show at the Grand Ole Opry. Grandpa had been promising it since we visited there last month. I was excited about that too, but nervous I'd get sick again. "One day at a time," I reminded myself.

Although my stomach was still a bit queasy, I was feeling much better now. Grandma started singing "Blue Ridge (Mountain) Blues" to pass the time. Grandpa and I joined in, and before we knew it, we were at the entrance to the reservation.

"This has been part of Cherokee homeland for thousands of years," Grandpa exclaimed. "Here is where I come from, and I'm dang right proud of it!"

****

BILL

After talkin' with Cathy earlier in the week and her tellin' me that she, Grandpa, and Grandma were drivin' to the Cherokee Indian Reservation and then to a show at the Grand Ole Opry, I was happier than David was when he brought down Goliath with a sling and rock. I knew how much I enjoyed visitin' both throughout the years, and was sure Cathy would have a good time. A family vacation with Grandpa and Grandma was just what she needed.

They were expected to be home tonight, and I was missin' her. I thought about givin, her a call, but it had been a long day and I was exhausted, so I went to bed.

Before fallin' asleep, I thought back on our partin' words before I left for training— *"I want our goodbye kiss to last forever, Darlin'!"* Just then, the train whistle had blown, signalin' it was time to go. *Clickety-Clack* went the wheels down the track. The dreaded moment had come. Havin, said our vows earlier that February day under the willow tree, we had promised to love and honor one another and never part.

"Lights out, Commandos!"

****

"Rise and shine, 'cause your behinds are mine, Boy Scouts!" yelled the Master Instructor.

Ouch! Callin' me a boy scout is worse than bein' slapped across the face with a leather glove. "Oh, my turn is just around the bend," I thought.

Jumpin' from bed, into the shower, then into my uniform, I headed out to eat breakfast. Was I hungry? You betcha! Grandpa once told me, "I can eat a whole bull, with the exception of his horns!" (Well, I'm thinkin' there's one more exception!)

"Halt, Commando," called the Master Instructor.

"Yes, SIR," I replied.

Aww, shucks! What had I done wrong now? Quickly stoppin' at the dining room entrance, I waited to be reprimanded.

"Relax, Bill! Your team members should be arriving soon."

"Team members, Sir?"

"Yes, the Commandant has handpicked you to lead six others on a Special Forces Combat Team mission once you graduate.

The mission is classified top secret. So, shut your mouth . . . understood?"

"Yes, Chief, yet how are we to eat?"

"Through a commando straw, because the food will be pulverized!"

"Jiminy Crickets! Grandpa told me, 'There would be times in my life when I'd have to stand up; yet shut-up!'"

"Your Grandpa's a wise man, Bill!"

****

I had already made an authorized phone calls this week, but I couldn't wait to call Cathy to share the news about bein' selected to lead the team. I ran down to the control room, signed in, then picked up the phone and dialed home.

"Hello! This is Bill . . . to whom am I speaking?"

"Hurrah! This is Grandpa, Billy. Stop bein' so formal! Now, how many bears have you shot since you've been there?"

"Nary a one! I gotta save my ammunition for the Viet Cong. Is Cathy there?"

"Yes, let me fetch her."

"Wait! Give my love to Grandma and tell her I'm doin' fine. Once I get home, we'll sneak up the mountain and drink us some Muscadine wine. Okay, Grandpa?"

"Sure thing! Please be careful, Billy. Now, here's Cathy."

"Sweet Jesus, I miss you heart and soul, Darlin'!" I blurted out before she even had a chance to speak. "I would've given my last pair of overalls to have gone with you, Grandpa and Grandma. Did you, perchance, hear Johnny Cash perform at the Opry, Beautiful?"

"Yes, Honey. And what's more, I sent down a request for him to sing 'I Walk the Line' and dedicate it to you. He did, and it was awesome. After finishing it, he gave you a salute. Did you know he spent four years in the Air Force?"

"Of course, and he's the best singer I've heard so far. Now, I must share this with you. The word is MUM. This is top classified secret. I have been handpicked to lead a seven man Special Forces Combat Team on a secret mission in Vietnam once we finish training here. It is an honor, yet risky! I'll tell you more when I'm home prior to bein' flown over there. Shucks, my phone time is up already . . . got to go now! I think of you 24-7 and dream of you nightly. Please give my love to all and God bless."

"Take care, my beautiful Mountain Man and hurry on home to us. You are always in our prayers. I love you more than I did before, and I'll love you forever!"

Tears began to roll down my face, knowin' we wouldn't talk again for several days. I quickly wiped them away before anyone else saw me. The pain of bein' long distance tore at my heart.

****

"Out of bed and listen up, Commandos! This is our first day together as a Joint Services Commando Team. For those of you who don't know, I have been selected by the Secretary of the Air Force to lead us on all classified missions in Vietnam after we finish training here. My name is Bill, an Air Force Commando and Explosive Ordnance Disposal Expert'. Please stand and identify yourselves."

"Mark, an Air Force Commando and Ambush Expert."

"Don, an Army Green Beret and Intelligence."

"Bob, an Army Ranger and Language Expert."

"Larry, a Navy Seal Master Instructor and Underwater Expert."

"Ken, a Marine and Intelligence."

"Chuck, a U.S. Coast Guard Strategy Expert."

"Thank you, my brothers. It is an honor meetin' ya! I have always tried to ask first rather than give orders to anyone. So please keep that in mind, okay? There will be times in our training that I will ask you to accept what we do here in Florida to be considered real as in combat. Should I give an order, do it! Follow it immediately or your asses belong to me. Do all of you hear and understand me clearly, Commandos?"

"Yes, SIR!"

"We could hear you all the way from the Smoky Mountains, Boss!" Larry remarked"

"From this moment on, y'all call me Bill! Where are we, Heroes?"

"A swamp in the jungle of Vietnam," Don said.

"Okay, then let's cross the swamp . . . and go get 'em!"

After a few minutes of movin' slowly through the murky water, grass, and smelly whatever, I halted everyone so I could determine our next move. It wasn't long before I heard Mark yell out, "Bill! Get out of the water quick! There's an alligator swimming towards you!"

Sweet Jesus, my feet have become stuck in quicksand, and I can't pull them loose.

"Please toss a real grenade on the gator, Mark. That's an order! Do it . . . NOW!"

CHAPTER 16

~ THE PREMONITION ~

BILL

Kaboom! The grenade exploded, and a large greasy spot appeared on the water. My face and mouth were saturated with pulverized gator meat. The worst part was the meat was tough . . . and I couldn't chew and swallow it down! Grandpa had told me when I was seven, "Billy, there will be times when some things will stick in your craw." Damn! *Did you always have to be right, Grandpa?*

"A salute, Mark—way to go, Commando! I owe you for throwin' the grenade on the gator . . . like a hot potato.

I guess you know you saved my ass, Brother."

"Of course I know! I saved the rest of you too!"

"C'mon along then. Let's sing a happy song and go on home. Home away from home, that is! It's been a long and eventful day, and we're all here to say, 'tomorrow is only a blink away.' HOORAY!"

Walkin' along the track to what we call our shack, I remembered crystal clear somethin' else Grandpa had said— *"Premonition dreams or precognitive dreams are an ability to gain information about an upcomin' event prior to it happenin'."*

I wondered why I thought of that, yet it got me to thinkin' back . . .

"How will I know if they are premonitions, or if I'm just dreamin' normal, Grandpa?"

"These dreams are not common," he replied. "They are a certain form, but please remember that not all dreams serve as premonitions."

Hmm! "Then are they real or just a figment of the imagination only appearin' in fairy tales?" I wondered.

As soon as we got to the shack, I removed all my gear and cleaned myself up. Bein' exhausted from the day's activities, I lay on my cot and slowly slipped into a deep sleep, like a snail on a trail of tomorrow.

****

CATHY

Grandpa, Grandma, and I were in front of the console TV watching Walter Cronkite on CBS. It had just been announced that the body of Jim Reeves had been found, along with his wrecked plane, about 220 miles from Pigeon Forge, in Brentwood, Tennessee.

"Dang, he was such a great singer," Grandpa commented. "Adios Amigo."

Immediately, Grandma started singing, *"Adios amigo, adios my friend. The road we have traveled has come to an end."*

****

BILL

Rat-a-tat! Heavy rifle fire sent chills up my spine. We quickly descended the ladder, then dropped among the body parts on the ground. How ironic that we and the Viet Cong guerrillas should arrive at the same time.

VA-room, VA-room! Two mortar rounds fell short, then exploded. The third fell among us, but didn't explode upon contact with the ground.

"Get down, Commandos! They are usin' delayed timers," I screamed.

Immediately throwin' my body on top of the mortar round, I yelled, "Haul ass, men! I'll wrestle this bear!"

VA-room! The round exploded. I felt a gapin' hole in my belly. Next thing I knew, someone was holdin' me.

"Oh My God! Why did you do it, Bill?" Mark asked.

"Because I was closest, brother! Now, my boots . . . get them off quick . . . because I don't want to die with them on!"

"They're off."

"Thanks! Now I gotta know . . ."

"Just ask me, Hero!"

"The two rainbow trout we caught in the Smokies . . . whose was bigger . . . mine or yours?"

"Why yours, of course, Bill! Can you believe that?"

"Could, but I won't, because you never lied well, Commando!"

Clickety-clack! I hear the train a comin' down the track to get me, carry me home . . . and never carry me back!

"Please tell Cathy, Grandpa, and Grandma that I love 'em, and I'm sorry I couldn't stay longer. It's time to climb to the mountain top; thank God for havin' touched my face . . and for sendin' down His most beautiful angel to walk with me— from place to place."

"My friend, even at a time like this, you're so damn dramatic!"

"Of course I am! I got that gene from Grandpa!"

The pain was intense, and my eyesight was blurrin' up. I was very weak, but had to keep talkin' before I couldn't anymore . . . and that was comin' fast.

"Ah, damn, this hurts!" I groaned. "Hey, hey, hey, I must walk alone now . . . on through the hallowed grounds. I can hear the sound of Taps echoin' across the headstones of our brave men and women who died in the folds of Ol' Glory. HURRAH! I salute them! It's been nice knowin' y'all, but I must run along now."

"Why are you always in a hurry, Bill? I have something else to tell you."

"Just write to me, Commando . . . and address it to God—I'll get it!"

As I slowly began climbin' the stairway to heaven, I whispered, "Oh, we forged the fires in the pits of hell; we burned, stumbled and bled. Yet, through it all we stood tall and marched on to fight another day." I smiled as I felt myself leavin' this world.

****

"Good Lord! Dot the i's and cross the t's . . . wake up, Bill!"

"Why are you yellin' at me, Larry?"

"That must have been quite an awful dream, huh? At times, you sounded like Roger Miller singing "Chug-a-Lug"!

"Oh, no! It was a 'precognitive dream'. We were already fightin' the guerrillas in Vietnam."

"Pass me the bananas, please! Kind of ugly fellas, yet hungry, right?" Larry chuckled as he gave me a quick jab on the shoulder.

"Geez! I almost forgot, I have one phone call remainin'." Jumpin' from my cot, I ran outside, over to the phone, and dialed the number. Cathy answered.

"Hi Beautiful!" I said.

"Yay! It's you, Honey. God just sent me a gift!"

"He sent me one some time ago . . . and it was you. Thanks for the cherry pie—yummy, yummy! I ate it all up, just like the big bad wolf and Little Red Ridin' Hood . . . remember, Darlin'?"

"Oh my!" she replied. "I'm so glad you enjoyed it. I'll make plenty more for you when you come home."

"Goody, Goody! Will I be sleepin' alone because I snore?"

"Hush your mouth, silly gander! You know you won't! Are you sure everything's okay?"

"As good as it can be, bein' so far away from you. Now listen up. I'm graduatin' next month, and I know you all are comin' for the ceremony. Afterwards, how about you and me goin' on a little vacation before I head on over to the battle zone? We could go to Panama City Beach. I've got it all planned out. We'll dine some place special, then get us a nice suite. That's where I'll teach you some of my commando moves; yet don't worry, I'll save the special one for dessert. My, my . . . the thought of you and me doin' things like we did under the willow tree keeps my heart pumpin' . . . and my pony jumpin'!"

"Behave yourself because Grandma may be listening! But I want you to know, talking to me like that, you got my body quaking, and my heart aching."

Love Long Distance

"Dang it! I don't know how much longer I can live without you. You are my Angel . . . and I LOVE YOU HEART AND SOUL! My callin' time is up, though, and I must go now, Beautiful. God bless, and give my best to Grandma and Grandpa."

As I walked away from the phone booth, an old bluetick hound dog came up to me, licked my hand, and whimpered. I growled at him, then yelled, "IT'S ALL YOUR FAULT! DON'T YA KNOW THAT?" It looked sad as it continued on. "Aww, I'm so sorry I growled at you and said those cruel words; the Devil had a hold on me!" The hound dog stopped, looked back at me, and smiled. "What a shame," I thought. "The poor old fella has no teeth; but that's okay 'cause I'll have him some dentures made tomorrow."

"Someone call the doctor because Bill's lost it!" Larry yelled out to our commando brothers.

"I lost it a long time ago when the doctor dropped me on my head at birth!"

****

CATHY

The thought of Bill going into the jungles of Vietnam made me tremble to the bone. I didn't want to cry while we were talking on the phone, so I tried to stay cheerful.

The next morning, President Johnson publicly addressed the nation regarding U.S. ships being attacked off the coast of North Vietnam. Our involvement in the war had suddenly escalated.

"Grandpa, what does that mean for Bill?" I asked. "He's going to be in even more danger with the war heating up, isn't he? Why's this happening?"

"Cathy, please don't worry none. Bill's got to go, as you know. Stay brave and positive for him. That's the best we all can do right now."

"We'll keep him in our prayers for God to protect him," added Grandma. She sadly looked over at me.

"*Dear God,*" I said, while on my knees before I went to bed that night, *"please make sure Bill's going to be all right . . . because he's the best of the best! As you know, I love him so, and I can't live without him."*

Love Long Distance

Afterwards I cried myself to sleep, then had a disturbing dream of Bill jumping on a grenade and losing his life. I woke up in a cold sweat and screamed for help. While looking upward and clenching my fists, I shouted, *"IS THIS A PREMONITION, GOD? YOU CAN'T LET THIS HAPPEN!"* Suddenly I felt a fluttering, soft as butterfly wings, right below my belly.

I'm not lollygagging around any longer. The time has come; I'm going to tell Bill . . . that I'm pregnant with our baby!

CHAPTER 17

~ STRONG CHAIN ~

BILL

Somewhere off in the swamp, I heard a wolf call for its mate. "Geez! It's only four o'clock in the mornin'," I said to myself, as no one else was awake. The black clouds in the northern sky rolled and tumbled, causin' the rays of light from the moon to dim even further. The stiflin' feelin' intensified with every breath I took. I kicked, tossed, and tumbled; then memories momentarily comforted me.

"Welcome home, Billy! Golly, it's hard to believe that you are 23 already. Seems like only yesterday you were just a little guy, maybe four or five, and I took you fishin' for the first time. You were so small I had to bait your hook and help you hold the pole; then when the fish swallowed the worm—we got it! Oh my goodness, it was a whopper too! I remember you sayin', 'Grandpa, I did most of the catchin', didn't I?' I was so proud of you, Billy . . . and I'm even prouder of you today. Please remember what I said here as you journey along the pathway to God."

I wish those great memories had continued, but suddenly, another disturbin' premonition flashed before my eyes.

I came home from commando training and saw Grandpa motionless in his bed. His face was pale, and Grandma was cryin' her heart out. Dr. Smith was there and he put his arm around her and said, "I'm sorry; he's passed away."

Grandma cried even harder, then asked, "Where's Billy?"

"I'm sittin' over here in Grandpa's chair. No, he can't be dead, Grandma; he's only takin' a nap. Once he wakes up, we're goin' fishin' in the old blue hole—he promised me."

"Billy, he's with Jesus now," Grandma said.

"Don't say that again, 'cause I don't wanna hear it!"

****

"Shame on you, Bill! Sleeping in, huh? Are you aware that you were having a nightmare? What is wrong with you, Commando?"

"It wasn't a nightmare—it was a premonition of my grandpa dyin'."

"You're having too many of those these days. I'm scheduling you an appointment with our psychiatrist. Of course after talking with you, he'll probably need counseling as well. But as for now, get your heroes herded up, go into the swamp, then kick ass! Oh, did I mention, that's not a premonition—it's an order!"

"You just did, Sir!"

The Lieutenant's command was crystal clear. Two of my basic senses—seein' and hearin'—were workin' great. As I walked along the bunks where my fellow commandos were sleepin', I felt pride jumpin' inside my heart. Nary a one of 'em would hesitate to give up their life for me, nor I for them. We're brothers, joined at the hip by STRONG CHAIN, and I thank God for his gift.

"What's a matta', Boy Scouts? Waitin' for mamma to serve you breakfast in bed? On your feet, Commandos; wash your tails, and whatever else smells, then let's eat!"

It was the crack of dawn, yet they all got out of bed quickly and stood tall and straight.

"Durin' our meal, I'll brief you on our training procedures for today," I continued. "From this moment on, and until we return here tonight, we must, at all cost, speak and act so as to make it appear that somethin' is real, even when, in fact, it is intense training for the harsh realities to come. The Senior Commandos here will play the 'pretendin' role' of the Vietnamese guerrillas in the swamps of Vietnam. The ammunition in our guns and explosives in the grenades will be removed; however, the caps will remain to 'pop and smoke.' The bottom line is to successfully complete our training, and earn the recognition of excellence in 'theatrics' from our Commandant. We also gotta know when to hold 'em, yet when to fold 'em too!'"

****

Rat-a-tat-tat! We fired our guns until the barrels were hot, but the guerrillas kept a comin'! *Kaboom!* We tossed our fake grenades, and some ran away; others lay bleedin', appearin' dead on the ground.

"Dear God! Will we ever stop killin' one another and live in peace with our brothers and sisters?" I yelled. "That's it, Commandos! Safe your weapons and let's go home."

As we walked back to our grass shack, I felt sad and all alone. Of course it all came with the package; it were as though I was takin' two steps forward, then slidin' back three. Aww, I'll be alright, because I'll call

Love Long Distance

Cathy tomorrow and share my innermost feelin's with her. I'll tell her:

If I could, I would catch shootin' stars right from the heavens so that you could gaze upon them every day. I would make a bouquet of a hundred dandelion heads to grant you a thousand wishes. I would spin gold and moonlight to give you starry wings.

I would gather wildflowers from a meadow to make you dainty crowns. I would ask the wind to whisper my love until the day it blew to you. I would make the world stop spinnin' just so you could watch the sunset for one moment longer. I would ask the sea to try and match the color of your eyes so that you might look upon the water and smile, then laugh.

I would tell the world to draw me a map so that I could find my way back to you. So when you hear what the wind has murmured, you will look upon your wings and see your flower crown, and you will find your way back to me. Then maybe one day I can hold you again in my arms and whisper the words myself...'I love you'...Yes, SOMEDAY!

"Goodnight, Commandos! It's gonna be a long day tomorrow."

I was dog-tired as I lay my head down to sleep, hoping for continued happier thoughts and no more premonitions!

****

CATHY

My sleep was disruptive throughout the night. I kept thinking of Bill and worrying about his safety. I dreamed there was a gigantic bomb exploding, annihilating us all, like the Lyndon Johnson ad for re-election that I had seen on television. At some point, I must've fallen into a deep sleep because next thing I knew, the warmth of the sunlight was shining on my face. When I opened my eyes and looked at the alarm clock beside my bed, I couldn't believe it was almost 10 a.m. I immediately jumped out of bed, which made me a bit dizzy, most likely because of my condition. I found my bearings and hurried to the kitchen. Grandma always had breakfast on the table for us by now. Why didn't they come and wake me up?

When I got there, I was surprised that it appeared Grandma and Grandpa hadn't eaten yet. The hickory smell of fresh coffee and the sweet aroma of Grandma's griddle cakes were nowhere in the air. They didn't tell me they were going anywhere; something must be wrong.

"Grandma? Grandpa? Where are you?" I yelled out.

"In here," Grandma answered. She was calling from their bedroom. I headed in that direction, and when I got to the doorway, my eyes didn't want to believe what they were seeing. Grandpa was on the feather bed, a quilt tucked up to his chin, and lying so very still. He looked pale and wasn't talking. That was so unlike him, because he always had a lot to say, even when he was tired.

"I think he's had a heart attack. He's barely breathin'," Grandma told me. With a handkerchief, she quickly wiped away the tears on her cheeks. She was a strong woman, so I knew she was trying to stay brave. "I've already called the doctor and he's a 'comin'. There ain't nothin' we can do right now but keep a watch over him and pray."

I ran to his side and dropped to my knees. I held onto Grandpa's cold hand and cried, *"GOD, PLEASE...."*

Just then the doctor arrived, checked his vitals, turned to Grandma and said, "I'm sorry, ma'am, his prognosis looks grim. Of course I'll do everything I can."

"What can we do to help, Doctor?" Grandma asked.

"Join hands and ask God for a miracle," the doctor replied.

CHAPTER 18

~ GRANDPA'S FOOTPRINTS ~

GRANDPA

I could hear everyone talkin' around me; yet I couldn't move or say a word. Lately I'd been havin' chest pains, but told no one. Earlier I had met with an attorney to look over my will. No way was I gonna leave Grandma without a penny in her pocket. Billy and Cathy would also need some money to start a family once he returned from the war . . . that is, if he returned.

Life's been good to me overall. I can remember the first time I laid eyes on Grandma. Wow! She was a beauty. Since then, I've seen her go from blond to gray, and she's still the most beautiful lady in the whole wide world to me. Why, I'm the luckiest man alive to have her as my bride. She's been by my side through thick and thin. She's put up with my flamboyant ways, my moonshinin' days, and my more than occasional cussin' and complainin'.

I tried to say as I felt myself slippin' away, "Where did everyone go, and why can't I hear you anymore?"

****

CATHY

"Grandpa's had a heart attack and there is some damage, although we don't know how much yet," the doctor said to Grandma. "We have to keep a watch on him in ICU for at least 24 hours and run some tests. Right now, he's just lucky to be alive."

"Oh my!" Grandma said as she stood by his side and looked down on him. She stroked his head and gave him a kiss on his sallow cheek. Grandpa appeared so frail and was unresponsive.

There was commotion as the medics came and moved him from his bed to the stretcher. Grandpa still didn't open his eyes. As they were headed to the ambulance, Grandma called out, "I'm comin' with you!" She turned to me and said, "Now you call Billy and let him know. He won't forgive us if we don't tell him."

****

My hands were shaking as I dialed the emergency number Bill had given me. After two rings, a stern voice answered.

"Hello . . . how can I help you?"

"Hello, my name is Cathy. I'm calling for Bill Bishop. We have an emergency here. I need to speak with him right away."

"Lady, this is a big place and I have no clue, offhand, who Bill Bishop is," the man replied.

"Oh, if you'd met him, you wouldn't forget him! Please . . . it's a matter of life and death."

"I'm sorry, ma'am, but if you aren't his immediate family, I can't help you."

"I'm begging you. Have him call me as soon as possible. He knows the number." I began to cry and the man's voice softened.

"Okay, tell me his name again. I'm not promising anything, but I'll see what I can do."

****

It wasn't long before Bill called back. "Hi Darlin', what's the emergency?" he asked. "Let me guess...you're havin' our baby!"

"How did you know? I haven't told a soul yet, and my doctor's not talking!" I quickly replied.

"That's a good one, Beautiful. I was only jokin' with ya."

"Ah...but Honey, I'm not joking with you! I was going to tell you, but then Grandpa . . . well, he's in ICU. He's had a heart attack and there's no telling if he's going to get through this."

"We can't lose Grandpa, especially with our new baby comin'! Aww, Darlin', keep strong for Grandma and try not to worry. I'll get an emergency leave to come home as soon as possible. We'll get his heart pumpin' again like new. Grandpa's made of strong chain, remember? So, I'm really gonna be a daddy, huh? Hurrah! I want to feel our baby kickin' inside you. Now listen up, I'll be there before you know it."

"I love you heart and soul, Bill!"
"Right back atcha, Cathy!"

****

BILL

Once I explained the dilemma to the Commandant, he had orders cut, and I was again homeward bound. Not havin' money for a bus ticket, I would hitchhike as I had done many times earlier in life. I grabbed my duffle bag, threw in the bare essentials, and headed out. Walkin' along the highway, I held my thumb up, smiled, then saluted the passin' motorists. All at once, the driver of a '64 VW Bus pulled off onto the side of the road and yelled out, "Hey there, turkey—gobble, gobble! Get outta that uniform and make peace, not war!"

"Damn it . . . just my luck. Another Greenwich Village beatnik lost in Florida," I said to myself.

I slowly walked up to the red and white bus, which reeked of marijuana. I reached out my hand, did my commando squeeze on his Adam's apple, then said, "If you ever call me turkey again, it better be on Thanksgiving Day. Now, by the grace of

God you're still alive, so haul ass and stop smokin' all that grass—it'll ruin your mind!"

As I watched him drive off, I brushed his comments away, and my thoughts returned to a Thanksgiving of yesterday.

"Grandpa! You promised me when I turned eight years old, you'd take me turkey huntin' on Thanksgiving. Well, as you know, I turned eight a while ago, and tomorrow's the day."

"You betcha it is, Billy! So, go do your chores, jump in bed, then get a heap of sleep, 'cause we'll be headin' out when the rooster crows at daylight."

We went huntin' early Thanksgiving mornin'. Each of us bagged a whopper, and Grandma cooked 'em for supper—yummy, yummy! The love we shared with one another remains etched on my mind.

"Geez! Come on back from yesterday!" I said to myself, "'cause you have a long way to go to be with Grandma, Grandpa,

Cathy, and our baby." At that moment, I heard a horn sound—turned around, and saw an 18-wheeler comin' my way.

"Sweet Jesus! What's gone wrong with that fool driver? He's lost control of the truck and is gonna run me over! *Why me, God?*"

I heard a thud, then felt myself tumblin' along the road. Although the darkness was walkin' across my eyes, I saw Cathy smile and wave, then I heard her say, "We're waiting, Honey—hurry along!"

CHAPTER 19

~ A LULLABY FOR BABY ~

BILL

"Wow! Quite a tumblin' performance there, Bill. I witnessed the driver of the 18-wheeler bump you. He did, however, do his best to avoid contact; so I would say, matter-of-fact, you're lucky to be alive. I'll report the details of the incident to the State Highway Patrol as a 'hit and run.' Are you okay now? May I help in any way?"

"First off, you can tell me who you are and how you know me."

"My name is Rick Woods. Most everyone calls me Tennessee. I'm a Navy Seal, and am two weeks ahead of you in class. On your last mission, I played the Viet Cong guerilla whom you shot in the keister!"

"Pray tell! Small world, huh? Did the plastic bullet sting your butt?"

"Sting? Ouch! What martial art training did you learn the tumblin' act in?"

"Taekwondo. Of course you wouldn't know 'cause it's not a requirement for Boy Scout training."

"Oh, I'll not go there at the moment. However, I will say that every commando knows how full of poppycock you are, and it'd take twenty boxcars on a train to haul it all away!"

"Well I'll give you this much—you know how to give it back. What part of Tennessee you from, Rick?"

"Gatlinburg. If you go any farther east, you'll be crossin' the Smoky Mountains into Cherokee, North Carolina. Know where it's located, Bill?"

"I graduated high school there. I was born and raised in Pigeon Forge, Tennessee. Presently, I'm on emergency leave to see my grandpa. He's had a heart attack and the prognosis looks grim.

"A coincidence, indeed! I'm headed there on a week's regular leave to do some trout fishin' prior to goin' to Vietnam. Just might bag me a big ol' bear while I'm there. Now let's figure this out. The distance from here to Gatlinburg, Tennessee, is 546 miles. Our travel time will be around nine hours. We'll stop off halfway in Atlanta, Georgia, and eat at Howard Johnson's Restaurant. It has great fried clams and 28 flavors of ice cream! Makes my mouth water just thinkin' 'bout it! So, c'mon, brother . . . pitch your bag in my vehicle, and let's ride."

"Thanks, Rick. Mind if I crash in back for a while? I feel like Elvis Presley when he was 'All Shook Up'"!

Sweet dreams, Commando! I'll wake you in Atlanta."

****

CATHY

"Cathy, listen here. Grandpa ain't respondin' to either one of us, but we shouldn't fuss 'cause he's a strong man, and I've prayed long and hard. I'm believin' he's just given up, temporarily. Soon enough, he'll be back on his feet again, givin' me another reason to swat him with my broom for misbehavin' and scarin' us," Grandma said, although she was still very worried. In all their years together, she'd

173

never seen Grandpa unresponsive and with tubes coming out of him. The heart monitor gave a steady beat, showing his heart was now working fine, but in her mind she was wondering if it was going to hold up.

"You did say Billy was a comin', didn't ya?" she asked.

"He is doing his best to get here as soon as possible," I replied. "Of course, it's a long journey. Still, I'll bet we'll be seeing him soon enough. I told him to come straight to the hospital because we'd both be right here by Grandpa's side. Why? Do you think something's happened to him too?"

"You know as well as I do that somethin's always happenin' to Billy! But he should be here any time now."

"I hope so Grandma. Grandpa really needs him, and so do both of us! Also, we've got some big news to share with you that might cheer Grandpa up."

****

BILL

Rick and I ate like Grandpa's hogs, then I drove on to Gatlinburg while Rick slept.

The miles passed like sand through an hourglass . . . and thank God, we were home. Rick dropped me off at the hospital. As I walked into Grandpa's room, Grandma and Cathy rushed over and gave me a big hug.

"Oh Honey, we've missed you so very much!" Praise God for the gift of compassion!"

"Yes, thank the Lord you're home, Billy!" Grandma exclaimed.

After the huggin', I walked over to the hospital bed and put my hand on Grandpa's forehead.

"I'm here for you, Hero! So, show your colors!"

I watched as Grandpa stirred and slowly opened his eyes. He looked into mine, then smiled.

"I'll be alright now, Billy, so don't you worry none. I was kind of tired after fightin' in the trenches for so long, that's all. A little bit of a setback, but I'll just take a short nap, then you and I will go fishin' and catch a heap for supper."

"Of course we will! While you're sleepin', though, I'll flirt with Cathy, then feel our baby kick."

"Aww, you silly gander! It won't kick until around seven months," Cathy replied.

"So that's the good news you were talkin' about," Grandma remarked. "Grandpa did you hear? Our Billy and Cathy are havin' a baby! Why that's wonderful, you two!"

"Yes," Grandpa agreed, although his voice was weak. "Now I need to get better, don't I? We can't have that great grandchild of ours growin' up without me."

"Seems like you just gave Grandpa a reason to keep on livin'! God bless your hearts," Grandma said as she looked at us. She blushed and quickly turned away 'cause I had Cathy's pretty dress lifted up so I could plant a big kiss for the baby on her belly.

"I'll teach it to kick when we get Grandpa home," I said to Cathy afterwards. "You can be sure of that. In the meantime, I'll sing to it."

"In your mamma's cradle, hush, don't cry.
Just close your eyes, dream, and visualize colorful butterflies flutterin' high in the sky,
while I sing to you this sweet lullaby . . .

In mama's cradle, safe and sound;
a beautiful miracle to all around.
Baby is drowsy, cozy, and fair;
Mama sits proudly in her rockin' chair.

Forward and backward, the cradle swings,
and though baby's dozin', it hears
me sing.
High as a mountain top, down to the sea,
no one's so dear as our baby to me.

Wee little fingers, eyes wide and bright;
yet all are still hidden and out of sight.
Sleep on, Baby; later on, kick your feet,
Soon I'll hold ya—I can't wait till
we meet!"

"My, my, how I've missed you, Honey! Why I'm sure our child loves your kisses and singing as much as I do. What a beautiful lullaby! But please can you lower my dress now? I don't need anyone seeing my white panties!"

Just then, the doctor came through the door. Cathy shooed me away and covered up. The doctor didn't notice because he was lookin' intently at Grandpa and Grandma.

Love Long Distance

"We've got the results of the tests we put you through," he announced. "Now which would you like to know first, the good news or the bad news?"

CHAPTER 20

~ MOONSHINE NO MORE! ~

BILL

"We'll take the good news," Grandma said. "So, out with it!"

"The good news is the heart tests came back fine. There's no need for any surgery, and you'll have no restrictions except one. However, if you don't adhere to what I'm about to say to you, then you'll be back here again. Next time you may not be so lucky."

"Please Doctor! Don't tell me that I can't take Grandma out to the barn for a roll in the hay no more! I promise you, although she's quite the demandin' sort, I can handle it. I'm made of strong chain, ya know!"

"Aww, Ol' Man. You know you haven't taken me in the barn for a spell now. Just as well, because you stay so full of moonshine, your breath would set the hay on fire."

"The truth be told!" replied the doctor. "No worries, a roll in the hay is okay, but moonshine or any other alcoholic beverage is to be no more. That being said, here's the bad news: You have an alcohol-related liver disease. Simply put, the disease is caused by damage to the liver from years of excessive drinking. In the final stage, the liver becomes inflamed, swollen, and can lead to death."

"Now I gotta hide all that moonshine and Muscadine wine I make so Grandma don't find it!" Grandpa started to chuckle, but the doctor wasn't amused . . . nor was Grandma.

"May I call you Grandpa as well?"

"Why of course, Doctor! Grandma over there has called me a heap of names. She's called me Ol' Man, Silly Gander, Moonshiner, and one time she even called me a 'Sorry Dog'; yet she called me to the supper table as well. Speakin' of, I can't wait to get back home to have a decent breakfast of Tennessee Pride Country Sausage, biscuits and gravy. Honestly, this hospital food tastes like . . ."

"THAT'S ENOUGH!" Grandma interjected. "Now you listen up and take heed of what the doctor is tellin' ya! There'll be no more moonshine or Muscadine wine for you 'cause you've reached your limit! But I'll tell you what . . . if you give up the spirits and behave yourself like you're supposed to, then a roll in the hay may, someday, be a reality."

"Hip-Hip-Hurrah!" Grandpa replied. "Now you're talkin'! You know, this Tennessee Mountain Man still has a heap of 'Burning Love' to give; 'course don't forget, the last time I had my way with you in the barn, you bit my tongue, and nine months later Billy's daddy was born."

I was listenin' to the conversation. Although Grandpa was jokin' around like he always does, I knew he was probably worried, and so was Grandma. However, laughter is the best medicine, so I decided to join in.

"Hey y'all! A salute, Grandma! So it's because of you bitin' Grandpa's tongue that I'm here today, huh? Hooray!"

Cathy was findin' it hard to be humorous. She knew Grandpa had a bad liver, so she started cryin' and quickly left the room.

"What's a matta' with Cathy?" Grandpa asked. "Don't she know I'm gonna be alright, especially since we got a great grandchild on the way? Now go fetch her, Billy, and set her straight while I spend a little more time talkin' with Grandma and the doctor."

****

"Darlin', where've you been? I've been lookin' all over for ya," I said to Cathy as she was walkin' down the hall toward the hospital room.

"I'm sorry. I was so upset thinking about Grandpa's condition. You all were joking, but it's serious, you know! I went to the chapel and said a prayer for him. Then I needed the restroom. My bladder can only hold for so long now that I'm pregnant."

"Yes, Angel . . . now come on over here and give your Commando a big hug and kiss before we go back and join Grandma and Grandpa."

"Honey, you know just what to say and do; I've missed you," she replied.

After kissin' her deeply, I held her body close against mine. She snuggled her head into my chest, and her arms were locked around my waist like she never wanted to let me go.

"Do you remember the fragrance of the letters I mailed to you?" she asked softly. "It's what I'm wearing now."

"Of course, how could I forget?" I reached around behind her and started to lift her dress again. "Are you still wearin' the white panties too?"

"Now you behave yourself!" she demanded. But then she chuckled.

HURRAH! I finally made her laugh, like I intended to.

****

"I need all of you here at Grandpa's side because I have some more good news to tell him," Grandma announced as we re-entered the room.

"Well, when you gonna tell me, Ol' Woman? Cathy and Billy are back, so c'mon!"

"Right now, Ol' Man. The doctor said that if you behave yourself, and mind what I say, he'd let you go home first thing tomorrow mornin'. Do you promise me you'll do so?"

"Golly Geez! I promise you . . . and soon enough, we got a hot date in the barn, don't ya forget now!"

****

We brought Grandpa home the next mornin', and I thanked God for the miracle. After eatin' the breakfast he'd been wantin', Cathy and I presented him with a Winchester lever-action rifle. I had found it at a pawnshop in Florida.

Grandpa picked up the rifle, did a shoulder salute, stood tall, smiled, then broke down and wept. After embracin' him for a stretch, I told him he'd have to go behind the barn, 'cause like he always told me, that's where men go when they don't want no one to see them cry.

Cathy then started cleanin' up. She washed the dishes, and Grandma helped her dry them. When they were finished, I took Cathy's hand, and we were off to the Red Cross to plead my case.

I explained my dilemma of gettin' back to my base after hitchhikin' here because of Grandpa's bad health. A Red Cross agent got on the phone, called my Commanding Officer, and spoke with him briefly. Afterwards, I was handed three hundred dollars—a heap more than I thought I needed for a train ticket. I wasn't about to complain. I signed for the money, thanked the agent, and we were outta there in a heartbeat.

I wanted our walk to last forever, but the train station was only two blocks away. Although our partin' would be such sweet sorrow, I'd be back in training with my commandos tomorrow. With a sad heart, I bought a ticket, then Cathy and I waited for the train to come down the track.

The iron wheels squealed to a stop, and the brakeman lowered the steps from the top. I climbed them one by one, then turned around, and saw Cathy standin' on the ground while blowin' kisses to me in the wind.

"We'll all be salutin' you soon at your graduation, our hero," she called out.

"Darlin', you are finer than a frog hair split three ways—yes indeed!" I replied.

Love Long Distance

"All aboard!" the conductor yelled. I walked inside, sat down, and waited. The assistant engineer began shovelin' coal into the engine combustion chamber, the brakeman released the brakes, and the train moved slowly away. Once again, I listened to the "clickety-clack" of the wheels on the tracks while we continued to gain speed.

As we drew near to an old wooden bridge over a "crick", I heard a deafenin' crash and saw the engine jump the tracks. I was thrown through an open window, made contact with the ground, then gazed at the engine all aflame in the muddy stream. I felt all alone. *"Please God! Awaken me from this morbid dream!"*

CHAPTER 21

~ THE OL' STONE WELL ~

BILL

"*Sleep, My child! It's Sunday morning down there already. Do you hear the baby birds singing and the church bells ringing? It's off to church you go. So, c'mon now—don't be late.*"

"*Oh, I hear You, God! I'm a 'walkin' along the pathway now. May I take a moment, call up to Jesus, and thank Him for lovin' me?*"

Jesus heard me and softly whispered down, "*Come, My child. Venture with me and see the awesome creations of my Father. Speak not of yesterday's hurt and sorrow; speak only of My promise for tomorrow. Can't you feel your knees shaking and bones aching? Hurry along now—supper's on the table. There's a chair for you at My side, and a chilled glass of wine for a toast. In God's Kingdom, no one gets old, but it's time to dine; supper's getting cold!"*

After eatin' our fill, I looked around and was surprised to see Cathy in the Garden of Eden pickin' an apple from the "forbidden tree." I was dismayed, 'cause she was cryin'.

"Don't you see my Angel is hungry also?" I said to Jesus.

"Of course I do! Invite her to My table too. Now be sure to fold each of her wings carefully, seat her, then say in your very special way, 'I LOVE YOU!'"

"Angel, why are you cryin'?" I asked.

"Aww, Bill. I was so sad and lonely, and I've missed you so very much. My heart was so heavily burdened. All I knew to do was ask God to bring me to you. He assured me Grandma and Grandpa would be all right, but I can't live my eternal life without you in my sight. Then again, I don't know if I fill you with delight, as you do me. I must hurry up and ask Jesus to reassure me. *"Tell me, Jesus . . . how can I know for sure that Bill's love for me is true?"*

"Easy answer, My child! Would I bring you both together, always to walk joined at the hip forever, if it weren't true? Believe in Me and this too shall pass—you'll see. Now both of you enjoy this gift of eternity."

I opened my eyes, looked around and found myself still on the ground. "What's a 'matta with you, Commando?" I asked myself. As I jumped to my feet, I could feel my heartbeat, like the little drummer boy *rat-a-tat-tattin'* on his drum. The train had gotten off the tracks; but there had been no crash. I had instead passed out when I hit my head. I was alright, though; I wasn't dead, and neither was Cathy! With my wild imagination, I had concocted the scene. Could it be another premonition or was it just another dream?

Love Long Distance

The railroad crew had been workin' to get the train back on the tracks; the rails were still intact. I grabbed my sack and went out to join the other passengers who had gotten off the train and were lookin' on. An hour later, once again the conductor called out, "All aboard."

I climbed the steps, found a seat, then fell asleep.

The remainder of our trip became history.

****

"Rise, shine; yet don't whine, children! Your mama's not here to cook your breakfast. So off to chow you go, Heroes," the Chief Commando Instructor yelled.

"Why did I feel that he was a rat fink?" I asked myself as I headed off to eat. It was a rotten job that he was shoulderin'; yet he loved it like Grandpa's hogs love slop.

"You were on emergency leave for four days, Commando, but I didn't assign anyone to lead your Joint Services Team while you were away," he said to me. "Being handpicked by the Secretary of the Air Force, you're the only one to lead the course. However, you've got a long way to go, and a short time to get there. So shoot your best shot, and let me see what you've got. Is that too hard, Bill?"

"Well, Boss! It'll be easier than killin' a Smoky Mountain grizzly bear with a mule's hair. Thanks for bein' there, Sir."

****

"Fall in, Commandos, and let's go kick ass!"

"Look, Bill! The Viet Cong is leaving the swamp, and they're heading for the tall grass."

"I see 'em, Roy. Shoot low, men, 'cause they're crawlin'. *Rat-tat-tat-tat* Hurrah! Way to go, Commandos! Betcha a whole bunch died in their boots, and many others won't be goin' home a walkin' or talkin' no more."

****

GRANDPA

I was relaxin' in front of the TV and started to wonder where she was at. I turned my head this way and that, lookin' all around, but she was nowhere to be found.

"Cathy, where's my ol' woman?" I asked.

"The last time I talked with her, she was planning on drawing water from the well to make us all some Lipton tea. Come to think of it, that was quite a while ago," Cathy replied.

It wasn't like her to be gone so long; she should know what time it is. "Why don't you go look and see if she's in the barn with our cow, Bessie.

Maybe she wanted some milk to go with that tea," I suggested.

"Tea with cream and sugar sounds good, but not as good as moonshine or Muscadine wine."

"Hush, Grandpa!"

"And Cathy, once you do fetch her, tell her to get in here real quick . . . 'cause 'General Hospital' is comin' on. She won't wanna miss it."

****

CATHY

I went to the barn and said hello to Bessie, but Grandma wasn't there. The old rooster was in the corner. He was strutting back and forth, kinda slow, putting on a show for a half-dozen hens. Head up high, he glanced my way, and the hens started clucking, as if to say, *"Come on over and watch this 'macho' display!"*

"I would if I could, but I got to find Grandma. Where is she?" I wondered, being in a near state of panic by now. "Oh, please! If you can hear me—answer up!" I hollered.

Suddenly getting light-headed, I sat down on the back stoop to rest. That's when I heard a distressful sound blowing in the wind. It was Grandma's!

"Help, HELP! I've fallen into our well! The water is up to my chin, and I'm freezin'. Hurry and get someone who can help me get outta here . . . FAST!"

Panicked, I tried to run, but kept falling. *"Oh my God! Please help me to help Grandma,"* I prayed.

CHAPTER 22

~ TROUBLE ONCE AGAIN ~

August 21, 1964

My Dearest Bill,

My heart hurts tonight. You've only been gone a couple of days, but it seems like forever. I miss you terribly! Grandpa, Grandma, and our baby miss you too. Soon we'll be coming for your graduation, and that will be a miracle from God. In reference to our baby, does the base library have books on infant and baby care—things like sterilizing a bottle, changing diapers, etc.? Just a thought because once it's born, I'll probably need your help at times. I'll pay you with kisses, okay?

Around here it's been kind of crazy lately. Right after you went back to Florida, Grandma fell into the ol' stone well. I looked almost everywhere, but couldn't find her until I heard her yelling for help. The water was almost up to her chin, and she was awfully cold. Grandpa quickly grabbed a rope and the quilt from the sofa. He tied one end of the rope onto blue mule's collar, then made a slip knot in the other end. He said it would make it easier for Grandma to put it over her head and secure it under her armpits. He threw it down to her, and although she was numb from the freezing water, she was able to grab it. Minutes later, she was standing outside the well, wrapped in the quilt, and giving Grandpa hell! She blamed him for her falling. I'd tell you the words she used, but Jesus is listening. Apparently when she went there to draw water to make some tea, she discovered one of Grandpa's secret hiding places. Down in the well was a bottle of his homemade moonshine. She reached down to pull it out, and that's when she fell in. So Grandpa's in trouble once again!

Grandpa has been making up for it all. Unless he's sneaking moonshine we don't know about, it seems he's listening to the doctor and staying away from it. He's been pampering Grandma since he rescued her. He even made supper for us that same night because she was at her wit's end and awfully sore. He's not a good cook, though. His version of cooking is preparing a boxed Kraft spaghetti dinner. He attempted to make some biscuits, but they were as hard as bricks. I was so glad when I saw Grandma back to herself again and in the kitchen the very next day. I'm sure Grandpa was too.

Now there's something else I want to tell you — I called my mother! She seemed surprised to hear from me, and the conversation was awkward at first. However, once I sprang the news about the baby, she was thrilled beyond belief. I mentioned that maybe if she was feeling *well, she could come down for a visit after it's born.*

As you know, your momma's been in North Carolina for the past several months staying with your daddy's sister who lost her son, your cousin, in the war last year. We're so happy she is returning home tomorrow and will be traveling down with us for your graduation.

I must close now, Honey. It's been a long day, and I'm exhausted. Please remember that I love you heart and soul—you mean the world to me! I can't wait until you are home for good after you've bravely served our country. I dream of the three of us—you, me, and our precious baby—laughing and loving in the meadow under the willow tree.

Hugs and Kisses,

Cathy

****

Love Long Distance

August 27, 1964

Hi Beautiful,

Your letter walked through the doorway of my heart, and I whispered to myself, "I thought of you today, but that is nothin' new. I thought of you yesterday and the day before that too. For every day, no matter where, I'll always think of you, and in my heart, you'll be there today, tomorrow, and my whole life through." Just know that I'm always here, lovin' and missin' you!

Today is Thursday, and our training is on hold due to Hurricane Cleo makin' landfall in Miami. It is the first to hit that area in 14 years. We are headed there tomorrow as a team to help with the clean-up.

Darlin', there are some events in my past that I've never shared with you, and I have a little time to do so now. Of course as you know, I haven't talked much about my father. He was Grandpa and Grandma's only son. The earlier years of his life were hard ones; yet he worked his way through high school and married my momma. They first met at the fall fair in Gatlinburg, Tennessee, and it was love at first sight. She told me he came up to her and kissed her without her consent. She slapped his face hard, and that only made him laugh. He told her she'd be his wife by spring. I can remember my momma sayin', "The birds were singin' and soon the church bells were ringin' when your daddy and I said 'I do' on April Fool's Day. Oh my goodness! I almost forgot to say, nine months later you came our way, and we thanked God for his gift." He joined the army before I was born. After Ranger Training, he was shipped over to France in WWII, and was killed in 1945, prior to Adolph Hitler's formal surrender to the Western Allies in May of that same year.

Even today when I say, "I love you, Momma," I can see a smile on her face, yet salty tears in her eyes. She was devastated when he died, and has lived with a broken heart since.

My daddy wasn't the only one taken by war. I give a "SALUTE" to my older cousin, a Navy Seal who fought and died in Vietnam. A headstone marks his place, *with his epitaph chiseled for all to know. God touches his face, and tiny flags wave hello. Oh yes! He pledged allegiance to Ol' Glory, then wrote his story. With bonded ties and misty eyes, he said goodbye to all. He did not die in vain. Oh no! He marched on to fame and immortality. Of course you also know he was my idol, and I miss him so.*

I'm goin' to lunch to eat a bunch, then love you my whole life through. Please whisper "I love you" to our baby too.

Forever yours,

Bill

****

CATHY

When I read the letter from Bill, I was relieved that he was finally sharing more about his daddy. Always thinking he was hiding something from his past, I wondered what it was. Now knowing how his daddy died made me understand why none of the family wanted to tell me, especially since Bill was also headed to war.

I was fixing to write him another letter, but soon after reading his, I was stricken with intense abdominal pain. Grandma rushed to my side, and Grandpa called the doctor. As we waited for him to arrive, we all joined hands and prayed, while Grandpa cried, *"Oh God, please don't do this to us! Take care of Cathy and our precious baby!"*

CHAPTER 23

~ SHADOW OF OL' GLORY ~

CATHY

My abdominal discomfort with intense suffering and near unbearable pain was causing me to toss and turn. "What is taking the doctor so long to get here?" I cried.

"Aww, Sweetheart! I don't know what to do to help you other than pray. The doctor is on his way and will be here directly," Grandma exclaimed.

"He's here now," Grandpa called.

"Please, come quick! The pain is excruciating. I'm so worried about the baby!" I yelled out.

As the doctor entered the room, he asked, "Have you noticed any bleeding?"

"No, I haven't. I hope that's good news."

"It sure is. I'm going to examine you, and then we'll see if you need to go to the hospital. Are you comfortable with everyone here while I do so?"

"If it's okay, I'd like Grandma to stay since she's a lady. But Grandpa, if you don't mind, I'm not showing off my behind, or anything else, to another handsome mountain man other than Bill."

****

The examination was through, and Grandpa was now back in the room. Everyone was anxiously waiting for the news. I was trying not to cry, but it would be a lie to say I didn't want to.

"Doctor, what is wrong with me?" I finally asked.

"Cathy, I know you're suffering; but I'm happy to say that there's no harm to the baby in any way."

"Thank You for the miracle, Jesus!" Grandma prayed.

It was such a relief to hear that. My biggest concern was to make sure the baby was fine. Still, I was in severe pain and didn't know what was wrong with me.

"Then why am I experiencing this stabbing in my abdomen, Doctor? I've got to get well again quickly so I can go to Bill's graduation in two days."

"Well, because you're pregnant in your second trimester, we're limited on what medication you can take for the pain. However, I will give you a safe analgesic, and I'm sure Grandma can make you some peppermint tea. I'll bet she also has a hot water bottle which will help you."

"I sure do," Grandma said.

"Good!" the doctor continued, "Now listen up, Cathy. You need to drink plenty of fluids, get lots of rest, and finish passing that kidney stone. Once you do, your pain will be through."

"A kidney stone? I should've known. I've had 'em before, and they ain't funny, are they?" Grandpa interjected. "I know what they feel like, Honey. May God bless and make you well. Dealin' with a kidney stone is pure hell!"

"It certainly can be," the doctor replied. "Hopefully that stone is small and will pass soon. I'll check on you again early tomorrow. If you're still hurting, we may need to help that kidney stone along in other ways. In any case, we'll get you well soon enough so you can go see Bill graduate. That's something I'll promise you."

****

The next morning I was out of bed as the sun reared its head. After around five minutes sitting on the commode in the bathroom, I passed the small kidney stone and was immediately relieved of the pain.

The doctor came and examined me, then exclaimed, "Good news! You are going to be okay. You may be a bit sore today, but that will go away." After he left, I said to Grandma, "This calls for a celebration of Muscadine wine, but Grandpa is not allowed to drink it, so . . . never mind."

"That's okay, we'll find a way to celebrate anyway. I'll make us a special supper tonight, and we'll all eat by candlelight," Grandma replied.

"Candlelight at night, well, that sounds swell 'cause I can always find my hidden wine in the ol' stone well," Grandpa yelled.

Grandma was getting furious. "Oh, so you hid wine down there too, did ya? I hope you're kiddin' Ol' Man . . . 'cause if you ain't, your livin' days are through!"

She grabbed her broom, ran across the room, and whomped him!

****

The day passed away, and so did any remaining discomfort. I started making preparations with Grandpa and Grandma to leave for the graduation. Right after our supper celebration, Bill's momma rode up in a taxi. The driver put her luggage on the porch, then she joined us in our quest to travel southwest, come early the next morning.

****

BILL

I jumped from the bed and said, "Up and at 'em, Commandos!" Old habits die hard, I reminded myself. After dodgin' nearly fourteen boots, it dawned on me that we had finished training. I seemed to hear a voice in my ear sayin', "I pray to God that your training was better than that of the Viet Cong's!"

Later on as the ceremony was about to begin, I said to my team, "So beat the drums and clash the cymbals 'cause it's graduation day. Now listen up, y'all! Stand tall, chest out, chin up, and eyes open wide. Is that pride I see lookin' back at me? Reach out, accept your diploma, then thank God for His gift."

Soon after as I walked up to the front of the stage, I glanced out across those in attendance, "SALUTED THEM ALL" . . . and called, "Hear me one, hear me all! We shall walk in the shadow of Ol' Glory. Some of us will stumble, others will fall, yet we'll pick ourselves up and keep on marchin'. We'll forge the fire in the pits of hell, then yell, 'God bless America!'"

I quickly scanned the audience and saw Grandpa, Grandma, Momma . . . and Cathy, the LOVE OF MY LIFE, as they waved to me. Of course our baby was growin' and showin' in its momma's belly. "Rock-a-bye baby; don't 'cha fear. Sleep peacefully, Little Angel, 'cause Daddy's here," I whispered to myself.

When the ceremony was over, I suddenly felt alone and blue, realizin' my training was through. After a short vacation with Cathy, it would be time to leave and fight, and there's a strong possibility that I might . . .not . . . no, I don't want to think about what can be! I jumped from the stage and joined my family.

****

The next ten days seemed to fly away. They were kinda like the pheasant I shot at in the cornfield when I was seven years old. Although I missed it and it got away, I didn't get mad 'cause Grandpa made me laugh when he said, "Golly Gee! There goes supper. I guess we'll just have an old cold tater—until later." Geez! Grandpa can be a silly gander at times.

Although I was fully awake, it seemed as if I was dreamin' like I did as a kid. Time was sure walkin' by in a hurry. I had made a one night reservation at the Eglin Air Force Base Guest House in Fort Walton Beach. It was for Cathy, Grandpa, Grandma, Momma, and me. After checkin' in, we went to a local BBQ shack in Fort Walton for the evenin' meal, then back to the Guest House.

The next mornin', we all ate breakfast at the Omelet House. From there, Cathy and I headed out to Panama City Beach.

After arrivin', we checked in for a five night stay at the Tyndall Air Force Base Guest House, caught up on a little lovin', then wined and dined at Captain Anderson's. I was also anxious to take her fishin' on his boat.

Grandpa, Grandma, and Momma drove in the other direction to Marianna. They wanted to visit the Blue Spring Caverns before headin' home. They had no problem findin' motel accommodations. Grandpa loves fast food, and has eaten at McDonalds for years, so that was their supper. After a restful night's sleep, all were ready to tour the caverns.

****

GRANDPA

"C'mon y'all! Climb aboard the ol' truck, put the picnic basket in my lap, and let's move out." I said.

"Yakety Yak! Don't you ever hush your mouth, Ol' Man?" Grandma was quick to reply.

"I can't, Ol' Woman, 'cause you're bitin' my tongue!"

"Aww, hog-slop! Will you never stop? Don't 'cha know Billy's momma is lookin' and listenin'?"

"That's swell—don't bother me none! Next time you're out in the field a pickin' peas, let's get naked, then go for a swim in the well, okay?"

"Oh my God! Why me, Lord? I go to church on Sunday, pray day after day that he'll change his way; yet the only thing he changes is his drawers on Saturday."

****

"What a magnificent sight to behold," Billy's momma exclaimed as we entered the caverns.

It was indeed. "What's a smellin' so good?" I said as I looked all around. My mind started wanderin' and imaginin' what it might be. Then I heard a sound . . .

"It's me, over here!" a woman's voice said. "I'm over behind the rock in the dark, next to a big deep hole."

"Oh, Baby—your perfume is tantalizin'! Please come a little closer so I can see ya better."

"Oh my, ain't you sweet!"

"Who's that you're talking to?" a man suddenly asked.

"That good-lookin' older fella over there with the silver hair. He reminds me of a teddy bear. But do you care?" I heard her reply.

"Of course I care, 'cause you're with me! Stay put; I'm goin' after him!"

"That sounds like a very mean and jealous man," I thought. "I'd better run as fast as I can."

I tried movin' at a brisk pace, but I have a bum knee, so the man kept gainin' ground. Soon his heavy footsteps were right behind me. His strong hand grabbed my arm and pulled me back. *"OH NO! Please God, I promise to behave . . . Now HELP ME ONE MORE TIME!"* I screamed.

CHAPTER 24

~ MARRY ME! ~

GRANDPA

"Wow! Quite a hard blow you just took, my friend. Are you alright?" the man asked me.

"Oh please, don't hurt me, 'cause I'm just a flamboyant and flirty ol' man. I didn't mean nothin' by it!"

"I have no earthly idea what you're talkin' about. I saw you hit your head on that rock over there. You looked dazed and confused, and you were sputtering some things I couldn't quite understand. Is there anything I can do for you? Do you need some help?"

"Aww, I was born confused and will probably die that way too! Yet I'm here today to say, 'I'm okay!' Thanks for your consideration and kindness."

"Excuse me, Mister, but I'd like my husband back," Grandma said as she approached us and pulled me aside. By the scowl on her face, I knew I was in trouble again. Ouch!

"He was just bein' kind and makin' sure I wasn't hurt. I bumped my head on that rock over there. Don't you feel sorry for me?"

"Not a chance! Don't think I wasn't listenin'! Now, are you gonna waste all your time chasin' women and fantasizin', or are you gonna join us and enjoy the caverns?"

"Do I have a choice, Ol' Woman?"

"Silly question! Now let's get a move on!"

****

CATHY

"Are you feelin' okay, Darlin'?" Bill asked as I opened my eyes to the morning sun and marveled at him lying there next to me.

Love Long Distance

"Honey, I've never felt better! Our baby and I are so happy being here with you. However, this week has flown by, and our vacation is almost through. I've been thinking about how hard it will be to say goodbye to you again tomorrow. I wish we were going back home to Pigeon Forge together so we could keep on waking up next to each other forever and ever." Right after saying that, I started to cry. Bill reached over and pulled me closer.

"Please don't you cry; our little separation will not be goodbye. Now dry those tears and let's hear some cheers 'cause I've got a wonderful day planned for us. We're gonna have loads of fun, you betcha! Whattaya say we start with me bitin' your tongue!"

****

Bill had a pocket full of activities planned for us and wanted to make sure we had time to fit everything in. After a quick breakfast on the base, we were on our way.

"First stop is Snake-a-torium!" he announced with a grin.

"You know I don't like snakes, Handsome! I have a strong case of ophidiophobia." My body started to tremble and quake.

"Fancy word for a fancy lady," Bill replied as he looked over at me and winked. "Now don't ya worry none 'cause I'll protect you. It's been open since 1936 and was the first tourist attraction in Panama City Beach, so we gotta go. There ain't just snakes there, either. They've got gigantic alligators and leopards too. And if you don't watch out, they'll come and bite your beautiful tail—lucky reptiles!"

Sure enough, they did have all those things and despite my fear of snakes, I even braved up enough to pat the python. I could tell Bill was proud of me! I thought we'd be done with reptiles after that, but the next attraction was "Ross Allen's Jungle Shows" to see more.

"The best is yet to come," Bill said as we left there and were about to enter "Miracle Strip Amusement Park" right next door. Now, looky at this awesome roller coaster ride! I can't wait to hear you scream when we get on it."

"You bet I'll scream! I'm sure glad I'm over my morning sickness."

"Me too, Beautiful! Now first, let's go play some Goofy Golf."

After putting around, we ate cotton candy and roasted peanuts, enjoyed the sights high up in the sky on the Ferris wheel, rode that roller coaster twice, and Bill played some arcade games until he won me a big stuffed bear. By the time we were done, it was already getting dark. I was exhausted and ready to have a nice dinner, then head back to the guest house. Bill insisted on one last ride, though. He helped me mount a beautiful white horse on the carousel and stood beside me as we went around and around.

"Why aren't you on a horse too, Honey? I'll be okay."

"Oh I know you will, but I wanna stay right here, 'cause afterward, I got somethin' to say."

When the ride stopped, he told me not to move yet. He went over to talk to the ride attendant and was back in a heartbeat. Taking my hand in his own, he looked into my eyes and told me to be prepared for a big surprise. Then he got down on one knee and asked, oh so sweetly, "Cathy, will you 'officially' marry me?" Before I had a chance to reply, he pulled a little black box out of his pants pocket and opened it. Inside was a beautiful diamond ring.

I was speechless. How could I talk? Of course we had already said some vows in the meadow before he left for training last February, and we always planned to 'officially' tie the knot when he returned from Vietnam. He even called me his wife occasionally; still I never thought . . .

"Darlin', don't you wanna?" He looked concerned.

"I Do! I Do! Of course!"

A big smile crossed his face before he whooped and hollered, "SHE SAID YES!" He got up quick and placed the ring on my finger. Wow! In one scoop, he lifted me off the horse and carried me off the carousel. A crowd had gathered and they were all clapping and giving their congratulations. I was so happy! We celebrated with dinner, dancing at the "Hang Out". . . and you can guess the rest!

****

It was the best of days and neither Bill nor I wanted the next morning to come, but it did. All too soon, he put me on a Greyhound bus to go back to Pigeon Forge.

Love Long Distance

He was leaving afterwards on a train to San Francisco where he would take a military flight to Saigon, Vietnam, and the jungles of hell. Once again, the tears fell as I waved goodbye to the love of my life. *"Please God, keep him alive!"*

****

BILL

As the bus pulled away, my heart broke into parts. "Please don't leave me, Cathy," I screamed. But she was already gone.

"Sweet Jesus! It seems that all we do anymore is say goodbye. Why, Lord? Am I to keep carryin' this cross up the hill all alone? Send me a sign so I may find peace of mind to do what I must."

****

I was lyin' down on the long padded bench after boardin' the train as my mind returned to the meadow, willow tree, and our little log home in the Smoky Mountains of Tennessee.

"C'mon Beautiful! Let's stroll through the meadow, Cathy. Geez! Do you see the little deer under the willow tree? It musta lost its momma 'cause it looks so hungry. Come on baby, we'll feed ya."

"Aww, Honey! Why did it run away? Will it come back another day?"

"Only Jesus has an answer for that, my Darlin'."

"Did you bring our blanket in your pack?"

"Of course I did! Wanna spread it on the soft grass, then cuddle?"

"Oh   yes! I thought you'd never ask."

I awoke to the *clickety-clack* of the train wheels on the tracks. My mind then moved forward in time. I prayed that our training was better than our adversaries'. The miles passed . . . and at last we arrived in San Francisco. The flight across the big pond became history, and we finally landed in Saigon. Sleepin' through the night, we were rested and ready to kick butt. An hour

Love Long Distance

later, we were in Bien Hoa, joinin' our fellow commandos.

"Hurrah!" we yelled—"Let's give 'em hell!" *Rat-a-tat-tat—Kaboom—Kaboom!*

Walkin' along, we stumbled, fell, bled; yet some lived to fight another day. Thank God I was still among the livin'.

CHAPTER 25

~ ABOVE AND BEYOND ~

BILL

Terrified by the rockets that were explodin' on our position, I yelled, "Dig in, Commandos! The bastards are firin' from the woods to our north." A near miss stitched my groin with fragments of shrapnel, thus knockin' me on my ass. The pain was near unbearable, my eyes were becomin' blurry, and I was feelin' faint from the loss of blood. *"Please! Don't take me now, God, 'cause I gotta get home to Cathy and our baby!"* Darkness walked across my eyes.

****

Sometime later, I awoke in the hospital at Tan Son Nhut Air Base in Saigon. Although I was still weak, the pain was much less, and I could stand on my feet.

"How long was I unconscious, Doctor? Will I be able to continue leadin' my fellow commandos?"

"That's not for me to say, Bill. You'll have to undergo a psychological evaluation by Doctor Miller. Colonel Rose of Commando 1 is with him now. I'll walk with you to his office."

After what seemed to be an eternity with a series of questions and an inkblot test, Doctor Miller finished his evaluation.

"Doctor, in your professional opinion, is Bill mentally alert and fit to return to his Joint Services Commando duty?"

"Did you say 'mentally alert,' Colonel Rose? Professionally speaking, Bill's overly theatrical in character and crazy as hell. In other words, he's 'Beaucoup Dinky Dau!" For example, I asked if he sometimes felt like kissing a Vietnamese pot-bellied pig, and he replied, 'Yes, but I'd wait until after dark so no one would see me.' Now please get him outta here before he aimlessly messes up all the inkblots."

"Bill, would you follow me back to your room?"

"You betcha! Just as soon as I thank Doctor Miller."

"Thank me for what, Bill?"

"For bein' patient with me. I'm sorry that I offended you."

"How so?"

"Doodlin' on them inkblots when I got bored!"

"Enough of your Smoky Mountain bullshit, Commando! Now get outta my office immediately!"

****

"Geez! Did you know that Doctor Miller is a religious man, Colonel Rose?"

"What makes you think that, Bill?"

"Because as I was leavin' his office, I heard him say, *'Why me, God?'*"

"Would you do something for me, Bill?"

"Certainly, Colonel."

"When you get out of the hospital and return to the killing fields, try talking with the Viet Cong before you shoot 'em . . . because they'll likely surrender to maintain their sanity! If I don't see you for a little while, happy hunting and Godspeed."

****

"Listen up, Commandos! We have a 2 a.m. drop-off. So synchronize your watches and let's get ready to kick butt," I bellowed. Havin' said that, I ordered everyone to climb into the chopper. Then we cinched our seat belts and waited for Captain Hill to haul ass.

"Are momma's little boys secure and ready to rumble, Sergeant Hopkins?"

"Yes, Sir! Now, get this eggbeater to the drop-off site quick."

"Why is that, Chief?"

"Cause these overgrown Boy Scouts are tying knots in my cargo nets."

Once hearin' that, Captain Hill slammed the engine throttle forward, then lifted the chopper straight up to around 600 feet in less than six seconds. Amazingly, no one lost their breakfast. Upon reachin' an altitude of 2000 feet, he switched the infrared sensor and night vision switch on, the navigational lights off, throttled back to around 260 knots, then headed north.

Glancin' at my watch, I saw the time was 1:30 a.m. "It's only thirty minutes to drop-off time," I called. Reflectin' back through our elite training in Florida, then forward to our mission ahead, I prayed that our training was better than the Viet Cong's.

"We're ten minutes out, Commandos. Stay buckled up until you hear from me, get your asses down the ladder, and take along the rest of you too!"

"Don't get so irate, Captain. Roy cut the knots out of the cargo nets."

"You know Roy is crazy, don't ya, Bill?"

"Of course. That's a prerequisite for commando training."

Hopkins laughed, shook his head, and remarked, "Every Sunday in church I pray that I will be spared from transporting commandos into battle. '*Forgive me Lord, where did I go wrong?*'"

"Aww, shit! There's a ground launched missile heading straight for us. Quick, Sergeant Hopkins, launch a flare to attract its guidance eye."

"Missile launched, Captain!"

"Cinch your seatbelts, Commandos, I'm rolling!" Slamming the throttle to full power, Captain Hill pushed the stick forward, did a power dive for approximately 1000 feet, pulled back on the stick, did a complete backward loop, then leveled off. The missile impacted the flare, then exploded.

"Hot damn! I knew the missile would miss us."

"How'd you know that, Sergeant?"

"Because I brought along my rabbit's foot, Bill."

"Why of course you did. Where is it now?"

"In my pocket."

"Then take it out and kiss it."

Once again, Captain Hill throttled to full-power; then dropped from 2000 to around 100 feet in less than ten seconds.

"You're plumb crazy, Captain. You could've easily aced the shrink's evaluation and become a commando too."

"Thanks for the assessment, Bill. Now take the stick, Lieutenant Hines, 'cause I gotta go piss."

"Geez! Welcome, Lieutenant. Slept in this mornin', huh?"

"No, just took time to eat scrambled eggs, Tennessee hickory smoked bacon, buttermilk biscuits, along with four cups of Maxwell House coffee. Have you eaten yet?"

"No, plowboy—I haven't! Guess what? If you get diarrhea, I hid your bucket."

"Heads up, Commandos! I'm dropping down to 20 feet and holding."

"Please, no more adrenalin maneuvers, Captain."

"Be nice, Bill, or I'll tell your momma you wet the bed. Now, get outta my chopper, babies!"

Quickly jumpin' on the ladder, we dropped among the body parts. How ironic that we and the Viet Cong guerrillas have arrived at the same time. Suddenly, a number of bright flashes, followed by an earth shakin' boom, sent chills up our spines.

A mortar round fired from a cave impacted the ground near our position. Guerrillas with fixed bayonets surrounded us, then began chargin' from all four directions. We fired our guns 'til the barrels were hot and our ammunition was history.

"C'mon, Commandos, let's give the bastards cold steel!" I yelled.

"What's a matter with 'em, Bill? They're running away like my old blue mule when he knew he had to pull the plow," Bob, a fellow Commando, remarked.

"Can't say, Bob! Only God has an answer for that one."

Love Long Distance

****

The day passed and the guns were silent. We were camped on a rock ledge about 50 feet up from ground level, takin' turns watchin' our backs while others slept. Captain Hill was gonna fly in early tomorrow mornin' with ammunition, food and water. I planned to write Cathy and give the letter to him to get it mailed. I took the first watch, then sat back to write.

September 30, 1964

Hi Beautiful!

Since I last saw you three weeks ago, I have continued to miss you, think of you, and love you more than a trainload full. Please whisper this to our baby too, okay? Although we're around 9,149 air-miles apart, my heart beats in rhythm with your own. I'm finally gettin' the time to write you, and I hope it walks the pathway to your heart.

The magnetism we hold for one another is filled with true love and peppered generously with passion. Nothin' compares to your little smile, cute nose, gentle touch of your hand when I'm feelin' down, and the green-gold of your eyes. My body is filled with you for days, weeks, months and years. You are the mirror of my days and nights. My goal in life is to feel our hearts beat as one while walkin' joined at the hip along the pathway to happiness, along with our daughter or son. So c'mon, Beautiful . . . and let's keep a walkin'!

Gotta go now, and face those who hate me. Please send up a prayer for me, as I shall for you and our baby. "Are You listenin', God?"

In closin', always remember, clickety-clack was the sound of the train as it rolled along the tracks takin' me away from you. Guess what? The same ol' train that carried me away is gonna bring me back alive as soon as it possibly can. You betcha! I Love You Heart And Soul!

Your Smoky Mountain Man,

Bill

CHAPTER 26

~ BABY'S A-KNOCKIN' ~

CATHY

I could feel my heart pounding. I tried to scream, but there was no sound. What was I to do? How was I going to make it through without Bill?

It was pitch dark as Bill and his Elite Commando Team jumped from the helicopter. They were parachuting into an area where the Viet Cong had been spotted. Their mission was dangerous; yet they had to get there beforehand, set up land mines, and demoralize the Viet Cong's fighting effort.

Bill knew what must be done. Everything had been planned out meticulously; and all was going accordingly. But while he was drifting down, the wind blew Bill's parachute shroud lines into the top of a tall tree; they got hung up on some limbs and suspended him about six feet off of the ground. Bill immediately cut himself free. His keen senses alerted him of impending danger, as he scanned the dark horizon and saw the Viet Cong already approaching. He quickly signaled his fellow Commandos to take cover and prepare to fight.

Suddenly, the Viet Cong began charging and rapidly firing their AK-47s. The loud, piercing sound of the bullets filled the air. Blood and guts were everywhere. A bullet struck Bill in the chest, knocking him to the ground. He tried getting up; but he could not.

Love Long Distance

With my body shaking uncontrollably, I woke up with a start. Realizing it was a nightmare, I tried to calm down; but it all seemed so real and kept playing in my mind. I wanted it to stop! *"Please God, don't let this happen. Keep Bill safe and bring him home to us,"* I prayed.

As I continued to lie in bed trying to erase all the fears in my head, Grandpa knocked on my bedroom door and called out, "Are you gettin' up, Cathy? The mailman just came and there's a letter on the table for you from Bill. Grandma's also gettin' breakfast ready.

A letter from Bill—YAY! It's been several weeks since we parted, and I've been worried sick. The daily news is saying that the war is intensifying; our troops are dying like flowers in the hot sun void of water. But, my strong and brave Mountain Man must still be okay. God willing, he will stay that way!

****

"Are you gonna share what he's written?" Grandpa asked me at the kitchen table. Grandma was serving us thick slabs of bacon, scrambled eggs, and buttermilk biscuits. She stopped for a moment because she also wanted to know. Tears were already flowing, and I could barely see.

"He's not sharing what's going on there; but he wrote me the sweetest love poem and told me how much he loves me and our baby," I replied. Suddenly I gasped in surprise and focused my eyes on Grandma and Grandpa.

"What's a matta' with you, Cathy? Are you okay? Did he say somethin' you don't want to tell us?" Grandma asked.

"N-n-nooo." I responded. "Would you believe that our baby knows what Bill said? Both of you, put your hands below my belly and feel your great grandchild kicking!"

Grandma rushed to the stove to set down the frying pan she'd been holding, then came back to the table. Both of them firmly placed a hand on my abdomen before another kick came.

"Sake's alive, I felt that one!" remarked Grandma with a grin. "Glory, Glory, Hallelujah! The baby's knockin', sayin', 'Wait 'til you see how beautiful I am!'"

"Oh My God, I reckon the baby's gonna be just like Billy—full of energy right from the git-go! Don't ya worry none though, 'cause when the baby comes out, I'll hold it real tight . . . so it don't get dropped on its head, like its daddy did."

"Cute story, Ol' Man," Grandma was quick to say. "But, you know that never happened to Billy. I was there helpin' deliver him, remember? You were in the other room celebratin' and drinkin' moonshine."

"Hush, Ol' Woman!" Grandpa replied. "Don't you go tellin' Billy now, 'cause he still believes it's true; he thinks that's how he got to be crazy enough to become a commando!"

For the first time in a long time, I smiled then said, "Our baby's gonna have the best great grandparents in Tennessee!"

****

October 7, 1964

My Sexy Mountain Man,

You are sexy, all right, as well as sweet and so romantic. How I wish you were here with me under the willow tree. You know what we'd do!

Of course we wouldn't be making no babies with our lovemaking, because we already got one cooking in the oven . . . and what a strong baby it is! Earlier today, both Grandma and Grandpa felt it kick. I wish you could've felt it too.

Your letter and poem really got to me. I was crying right from the start as I could hear your voice reciting the words, see your beautiful face, feel your warm embrace . . . although it's not the same as if you were really here now, is it? I fear for your safety and pray to God every day that He will continue to protect you.

Yesterday I went downtown to the record shop. The clerk there told me about the song, "You Really Got Me," just released by The Kinks. I played it on their turntable, and it made me want to dance; so I bought their new album. I've since listened to it several times on a new Magnavox stereo Grandpa surprised me with when we got back from Florida. I was really sad and blue after parting with you; he was hoping it would cheer me up. He's made it known, however, that he doesn't particularly care for rock 'n roll. 'Listen to some good music, like Jim Reeves,' he keeps suggesting. Someday I'll surprise him!

I'll close this letter with a poem for you. I hope you like it, Honey.

BABY'S A-KNOCKIN'!

For the first time in my life, I've found
true love.
It was granted to me by Almighty God
above.
Tho' you're flamboyant, histrionic and
flirty;
I knew, immediately, we were meant to
be.

Conceiving our baby, we've now become
three.
Although far apart, we're still a family.
Our child and I await your safe return.
While waiting for your hugs and kisses I
yearn.

Someday, not far away, we'll again be

together,
singing happy songs like birds of a
feather.
You'll make a weeping willow cradle for
rockin';
Hurry home, Honey, 'cause baby's a-
knockin'!

Honey, I miss you terribly, and worry so much about you there in harm's way. Please take care and promise to come home to me, our beautiful baby, Grandpa, Grandma, and your momma, too. I LOVE YOU HEART AND SOUL! God Bless.

"HKAYK!"

XOX

Cathy

****

Hurrying to the mailbox before the rural carrier came, I put my letter to Bill inside and raised the flag. Just as I re-entered the log cabin, the telephone rang. Grandpa answered, and I could tell by the look on his face that something was wrong.

"Yes, I'm family—I'm Billy's Grandpa! So, who are you?" He put his hand over the mouthpiece, looked my way and whispered, "It's the Red Cross from Vietnam, Cathy."

"Oh my God, something awful has happened to Bill!"

CHAPTER 27

~ SEND UP A PRAYER ~

BILL

I awoke in a hospital screamin', *"Dear God, tell Cathy that I'll always love her and our baby! Are You listenin', Father?"*

"Nurse! Please administer Bill a sedative . . . quick!"

"Ouch! You could've stuck that 3-inch needle in my arm rather than my butt, you know."

The sedative acted faster than my old blue mule ran to catch his girlfriend before she could jump the picket fence. The pain in my body seemed to be hauled away in a train, and the clouds in my eyes returned to the sky.

"Do you know where you are, Bill?"

"Of course, Doctor! I'm in bed, you silly gander! You sound like my shrink did when he walked inside my head."

"Just so you know, Commando, you're in the hospital at Bien Hoa Air Base. I'm notifying the American Red Cross, and they will contact a member of your immediate family back in Tennessee. Of course, you know God was fighting alongside you when you were shot in the chest, don't you?"

"Was He really? How do you know this?"

"Because He guided the bullet into the armor vest you were wearing, thus saving your ass and the rest of you too! Why? Because He's not ready for the likes of you yet, nor is Jesus. Although the velocity of impact was devastating, it only shattered an upper rib and threw you into shock. Your commando brother thought you were dying when he held your head in his lap."

"Were any of my brothers injured or killed?"

"One injured; but no fatalities."

"Hmm! Maybe neither God, nor Jesus, was ready for the likes of them either. So when are you releasin' me? The Air Force is not payin' for my vacation in this hospital. I feel fine, and all I'll need to go kick ass is a glass of Muscadine wine and a letter from Cathy."

"Thanks for reminding me. A letter from Tennessee was forwarded to you here yesterday. It's in the office. I'll have the nurse fetch it for you, okay?"

"Hurrah—a salute to you, Doctor! Oh by the way, may I ask what your name is?"

"Of course you may; however it's against the rules for hospital personnel to give their names to patients. So just call me Doc."

"You betcha, Doc! Now once again, when are you releasin' me?"

"Within a couple of days or so. I'll let you know. However, if you ever call me a 'silly gander' again, then you'll be here forever!"

****

The nurse brought me Cathy's letter. As I read it, I yearned to be holdin' her in my arms and makin' sweet love to her. When would those days come again? Would they ever? Although I promised her I'll return home unharmed, I sometimes fear I may never make it through this assignment alive.

Twice now I've come close to dyin'; yet God saved me. Is it because Cathy and my family are prayin' hard for me? I may be a commando, appearin' strong and brave, but the Viet Cong are also strong and determined to cut my throat—Ouch!

I've already seen so many casualties, and although I do my best to keep the morale of my fellow commandos high, inside I cry for all this unnecessary loss of life in the face of evil. Why is it we can't live up to what the Bible says—lovin' one another as we love ourselves?

"Pride and greed are of the devil," my Grandpa has often said. He also told me before I left for this hellhole, "Fight for the freedom of our country, 'cause I'm proud of you!" Could both, at the same time, be true? I believe so, although I still hold inside my sorrows for all this unnecessary loss of life.

I fear that even if I do make it home to Cathy and our baby, I will never be the same again. In order to do so, I shall cover my heart with callouses to protect it from breakin', as I walk among the dead with my head hung low. No one will ever truly know why God allows this.

Courage doesn't always roar; but the followin', written by Francis Scott Key, reminds me to remain brave as I fight for the freedom of my country and Ol' Glory.

~The Star-Spangled Banner~
Francis Scott Key

O! say, can you see, by the dawn's early light,
What so proudly we hailed at the twilight's last gleaming:
Whose broad stripes and bright stars through the perilous fight,
O'er the ramparts we watched were so gallantly streaming,
And the rocket's red glare, the bombs bursting in air,
Gave proof through the night that our flag was still there;

O! say, does that Star-spangled Banner still wave
O'er the land of the free and the home of the brave?

Love Long Distance

On the shore, dimly seen through the
mists of the deep
Where the foe's haughty host in dread
silence reposes,
What is that which the breeze, o'er the
towering steep,
As it fitfully blows, half conceals, half
discloses?
Now it catches the gleam of the morning's
first beam—
In full glory reflected, now shines on the
stream;

'Tis the Star-spangled Banner, O! long
may it wave
O'er the land of the free and the home of
the brave.

And where is that band who so vauntingly
swore
That the havoc of war and the battle's
confusion,
A home and a country should leave us no
more?
Their blood has washed out their foul
footsteps' pollution.
No refuge could save the hireling and
slave.
From the terror of flight or the gloom of

the grave!
And the Star-spangled Banner in triumph
doth wave
O'er the land of the free and the home of
the brave.

O! thus be it ever when free men shall
stand
Between their loved homes and the foe's
desolation;
Bless'd with victory and peace, may our
Heaven-rescued land
Praise the power that hath made and
preserved us a nation.
Then conquer we must, for our cause it is
just—
And this be our motto – "In God is our
trust!"

And the Star-spangled Banner in triumph
shall wave
O'er the land of the free and the home of
the brave.

Cathy's letter had walked the pathway
to my heart. I tried to swallow; yet the
loneliness I felt for her and our baby stuck
in my throat. Just then, a tear came to

mind, my eyes became blurred, and I reflected on an earlier scene in my life.

"Billy, what's a matta' with you, my little man? Don't you remember me tellin' you, 'Grown men don't cry?'"

"But Grandpa! I'm not a grown man; just a little boy."

"Hmm! Then go out behind the barn so no one will see you cry."

"Why? Cause Jesus wept that day, too!"

"Okay, go on and play, then later we'll go fishin'. At the table with Jesus there's a heap of little angels who love the taste of fresh fish."

"Aww, Grandpa . . . the whopper broke my fishing line!"

****

"Good mornin', Doc! Why are you smilin'? Do you have some good news for me?"

"I sure do! I have you scheduled for an appointment with Dr. Miller at 2 p.m. for a psychological evaluation to determine if you are mentally fit to once again lead your team in combat. Physically you are fit, and if all goes well with him, I shall be discharging you tomorrow."

After the evaluation, Dr. Miller found me to be mentally fit for combat, yet still crazy as hell. Of course I quickly replied, "That's a prerequisite to becomin' a commando."

I left the hospital and returned for orders. It was good to be back, totin' my pack. I was ready to again lead my elite team into combat.

****

"Long time no see, Boss! I hope you have an excitin' mission for us Boy Scouts."

"Golly Gee! Are you mad at me, Bill? Please call me Colonel Rose or Commando 1, because if you call me 'Boss' one more time, I'm going to take your Boy Scout cookies back."

"That's 'Girl Scout cookies,' Boss! Now the Air Force didn't spend a million dollars on my specialized training just to have me sit around and not kick ass. So, do you have a job for me, Sir?"

"Be in my office at 0:500 hours tomorrow morning (that's 5 a.m.), and I'll brief you on the mission."

Like sand through an hourglass, the night passed. Colonel Rose briefed me, and I was on the way to fight another day.

****

"Get down, Commandos! There's movement up ahead in the tall grass. So load, get ready to fire, then wait for my signal."

"Sweet Jesus! I see children, Bill; what are we to do?"

"Put your weapons on safe and stay down. The children are most likely Viet Cong sympathizers with plastic explosives strapped on their backs."

"Look, Boss! A small boy and girl are running toward us. They are smiling and waving, and they do have explosives strapped on their backs. What next?"

"Send up a prayer asking God to stop them! Otherwise, we're gonna hafta shoot 'em!"

CHAPTER 28

~ A MIRACLE ~

BILL

The little boy and girl kept on runnin' toward us. Of course both of 'em knew they better do as told. Maybe they were promised that they'd become angels in heaven where they could eat gallons of ice cream with candied cherries on top.

It was heart-wrenchin' to think we'd hafta shoot those innocent kids if they didn't turn back. They didn't stop despite our warnings. They were gettin' so close that I could see their precious little faces crystal clear. I raised my eyes toward the sky, then cried, *"God, have mercy on Your little children and tell them to go back from whence they came."*

"Get on home," I yelled, then slowly tightened my finger on the trigger of my M-16 rifle.

Suddenly, two of our ground support aircraft flew in from the north . . . *Rat-a-tat-tat—Kaboom—Kaboom!* Once the smoke and debris had cleared away, I called to my fellow commandos, "Is everyone okay?"

"Yes, Sir! We're fine as huckleberry wine; yet the little boy and girl are nowhere to be found."

"Lord have mercy! Is the Great Harry Houdini amongst us here today? Did he say, '*Poof,*' then make the little children disappear?"

"Wait . . . Sweet Jesus! Look over yonder behind that huge boulder, Bill. It certainly looks like the children lying behind it. Can you see 'em?"

"Of course I can! Now c'mon—let's move it, Commando, 'cause they may still be alive."

"But how in heaven's name could they have gotten over there, Boss?"

"My guess is the bomb explodin' threw them there; but the detonators strapped to their backs didn't activate."

"Sounds like a miracle, Bill."

"Of course it was, Mark, 'cause God sends 'em down for his little children."

At that moment, Mark placed a knee upon the ground, raised a hand toward heaven, then cried out, *"Glory, Glory— Hallelujah!"*

****

While I was sleepin' that night with one eye open, Cathy and our baby were heavy on my mind and deep inside my heart. When I woke early the next mornin', I wrote them a poem, not knowin' whether or not it would make it back home.

OL' GLORY!

We stand in the shadow of Ol' Glory, we're ready to fight today.
Side-by-side, with tons of pride, we're alone on foreign ground.
I say a prayer for you and our baby; so near in mind while away.

Love Long Distance

Knowin' you're back home for me muffles
war's horrid sound.

Quietly waitin', yet anticipatin', the Viet
Cong's on their way.
I think back to our last kiss and the
clickety-clack of the train.
Wavin' goodbye; tears in our eyes; I
promise to return one day.
But within our hearts, miles apart, we
must bear the lonely pain.

Suddenly, in the dark of night, somethin'
glitters nearby as I hear
the earth-shakin', blood-curdlin', gut-
wrenchin' noises resound.
Rat-a-tat-tat—Kaboom—Kaboom! The
enemy has arrived and is near.
"Down Commandos! Load and lock; the
guerillas are all around."

"C'mon men! Let's move, show the colors,
then kick butt once again.
Let's rumble, give them the cold steel,
and show 'em how we fight.
Hurrah! Shoot 'em all, and bring this
slaughter quickly to an end.
Ho Chi Minh! Your guerillas are history;
'cause we'll win tonight!"

"My Darlin', please don't worry, although
the loneliness still nips.
Let your mind erase all of war's disgrace,
and what I gotta do.
Just hold me steadfast in your heart, with
my kisses on your lips.
As promised, even if I die in battle, my
spirit shall return to you."

"Damn the torpedoes full speed ahead!"
Quote: David Glasgow Farragut

****

CATHY

It has been almost a month since we received the call from the Red Cross about Bill's injury, and we were all thankful he was all right. However, except for a quick confirmation that he'd been released from the hospital, we haven't heard a word since. I know he told me there would be long stretches of time when he couldn't get my letters, nor write one to me; still I worry and pray every day for his safety.

Love Long Distance

Last week, by a landslide, President Johnson won the presidential race against Barry Goldwater. I fear he will continue to escalate the conflict in Vietnam.

There was an assault by the Viet Cong at an airport in Bien Hoa. Then there were two typhoons in a row devastating parts of North and South Vietnam with thousands declared dead. Dreadful thoughts keep spinning within my head. The entire country is only three times larger than the State of Tennessee. How can it be that Bill is going to make it through all this, especially since he's already been injured two times? There are many months to go before he can come back home, and every day feels like an eternity without him here.

The baby is getting strong, and I'm already seven months along. My little "innie" belly button Bill loves so much will soon become an "outie, because my belly is already stretching, growing, and I'm definitely showing. Everyone around us knows now. There aren't any secrets kept in this small town.

Every night before I turn out the light, I sing the Supreme's "Baby Love" to our little angel while trying not to cry over being separated from Bill. *"Oh baby love, my baby love, I need you, oh how I need you."*

Although trying to sleep, I continued to weep. The golden rays of an eastern sun started to creep through my window. The old red rooster on the picket fence began to show his masculinity and crow. I smiled, but my heart was breaking. I wondered, "Will Bill be critically injured, killed, or become a political pawn in a game far beyond? Will I be left at home, all alone, with a baby whose father is missing in action*? "Please God! Have mercy on Your children, and protect him."*

****

BILL

The poem for Cathy was safely in my back pocket. I hadn't been able to send it to her yet and to also assure her I was alright. It had been close to a month of constant battlin' with the horrors of war embedded in my mind. The only joy to be found among us commandos, both in the air and on the ground, were the moments we could enjoy a nice meal, good American cigarette and, occasionally, a few shots of whiskey to numb us even more than we already were.

We'd shoot the breeze with one another durin' these sparin' moments and talk about when we would finally get to go back home to our loved ones. Course, we all knew deep down that many of us would die in battle before then, but those were sad thoughts, so we did our best not to think about 'em.

We were engaged in one of those moments when the moon was high and we were layin' low in our foxholes. My fellow commando, Don, was on watch. All was quiet and I was thinkin' the night might be peaceful, but then a sudden rustlin' woke us up.

The Viet Cong had crept up, and they were fast upon us. One pointed his gun down at Mark, ready to execute him. *Rat-a-tat-tat!* I took him down. We fired our guns, yet the battle wasn't won. There were at least a hundred of them, but only seven of us. "Shoot low, Commandos, 'cause some are crawlin' on the ground." I remember prayin', *"Dear Lord, if it's not askin' too much, would You send down another miracle? Would Ya, huh?"*

CHAPTER 29

~ RESOUNDIN' TAPS ~

BILL

Rat-a-tat — Kaboom — Kaboom! "Shoot 'em full of holes, so they'll not hold sourmash whiskey, Commandos. Keep your guns a blazin' and Ol' Glory a wavin'."

Kaboom! A mortar round landed directly among us, yet did not explode. "Get down, men! The guerrillas are usin' delayed fuses."

Mark immediately threw himself upon the mortar, then he yelled, "Haul ass, Commandos, 'cause I paid my insurance before leaving base." A moment later, the mortar exploded. Quickly movin' to his aid, I sat down, held his head, and saw a gapin' hole in his stomach with blood and guts everywhere. *"Why, God? Were You out of miracles?"* I called.

"Why did you do it, Mark?" I questioned as I looked down at him, tryin' to hold my composure.

"I was feeling guilty, Bill."

His voice was weak, so I got closer to him.

"About what?" I asked.

"Kissing your girlfriend in school. My boots . . . get 'em off."

"They're off! Want morphine?"

"Don't do drugs, remember?"

"Of course I do. I also remember you catchin' my big ol' bass when I was out behind the tree takin' a pee."

Mark looked up, faintly smiled, then slowly closed his eyes.

I suddenly recalled an earlier premonition, and screamed, *"Why God? This was supposed to happen to me!"*

The sound of Taps played in my head, knowin' my good friend and fellow commando was now dead, leavin' behind a beautiful wife and daughter.

The medics came, takin' Mark's remains. Later I would prepare for his funeral, but right now we were still in a battle, and I feared we would all die anyway since we were outnumbered.

God must've heard me ask for that second miracle, though, 'cause again I heard the sounds of the planes comin' from behind. They flew in low, shootin' rounds of ammunition at the Viet Cong. We weren't outnumbered for very long. Many died in front of our eyes, while others retreated. For the second time today, by God's grace, we weren't defeated.

Damn! I can't succumb to this slaughter. I must survive somehow, for just a little while more, then get home to Cathy and our baby. They need me, like Mark's family needed him. If I were to keep score, the agonies of the war would beat my faith into the ground forevermore.

I didn't know where to begin to regain my belief. The world bein' so unkind, darkness raced across my mind. *"God, why did You let this happen? If we're only meant to die, what's the sense in bein' alive?"*

I knew I'd never be the same with all I've seen and done since comin' to this bloody jungle. Sure, in boot camp and training we played war, but this was the real McCoy. I may survive the bullets, but will I ever survive the horror? Maybe Mark was the lucky one. No longer would he have to live within these gates of hell and hear the *Rat-tat-tat—Kaboom—Kaboom.*

****

All was deathly quiet later that night. The fightin' had stopped for a while. No one on our team could muster a smile. There was nothin' to be happy about. I lay down in my make-shift bed with my rucksack under my head. Tears burned my eyes as I asked again, *"Why, God, Why?"* This time, He replied, *"My child, I'll explain later, because you're busy now."*

When I finally was able to sleep, a vision came to me—such an unexpected comfort. It was Cathy in my dreams. Her warm embrace filled up the space within my grievin' heart.

God then spoke again, *"Although your heart may bleed, don't lose your will. When in doubt, know I am here and your family is back home for you. Hold fast to your faith—it will see you through."*

****

CATHY

"Cathy, keep lookin'. We've got to find the right one before nightfall."

As I walked through the woods with Grandpa, a cool breeze nipped at my cheeks while we searched for the perfect Christmas tree. Big, beautiful snowflakes began falling and soon the ground became a blanket of soft white. It reminded me so much of winters in New Hampshire. For a moment, a feeling of homesickness crossed my mind as the baby kicked within my womb. "No worries," I reassured myself. "Mom will be joining us for a visit when this little one is born not long after Christmas. Besides, there's no place I'd rather be than here, but it sure would be nice if Bill were here too."

We had heard from Bill by shortwave radio on Thanksgiving Day, but nothing since. Now, only a day away from celebrating the birth of Christ, I prayed he was still all right.

"Since Billy was old enough to walk, he would come with me every year to cut down a tree," Grandpa continued. "I sure do miss him!"

Love Long Distance

"I miss him too," I replied, "but thank you for convincing Grandma that I could take his place this time, even though I'm eight months pregnant. Look at me! I'm waddlin' through the snow like a penguin. I'm sorry I'm slowin' you down."

"You're still a pretty sight, and I'm glad you're with me. Have you ever axed down a tree? If not, I'm gonna show you how. Then once we drag it home, we'll decorate it and enjoy hot cider, along with some cookies Grandma's makin'. Course, I may even indulge in a little moonshine, too, but don't you go tellin' on me."

Before I tried to remind him he shouldn't be drinking that stuff, Grandpa pointed and shouted, "THERE IT IS! A beautiful Fraser fir, and the best Christmas tree in Eastern Tennessee!"

****

After supper, Grandpa pounded the base of the stand into the bottom of the tree and placed it in the corner of the living room. We strung multi-colored lights on it, then adorned it with fragile glass ornaments that had been in the family for generations. We all wanted to hurry so we could watch some Christmas shows on television.

When Grandpa handed me the star for the top, Grandma said, "STOP! There ain't no way I'm lettin' Cathy climb on a chair to put the star up there!"

"I'll be all right, Grandma," I replied. But then something happened. A warm liquid began running down my legs and onto the floor. "Oh my God, my water just broke!"

CHAPTER 30

~ CHRISTMAS SURPRISE ~

CATHY

A sudden, overpowering feeling of fear entered my mind. I was anxious, became sweaty, and began having palpitations. Once again I screamed, "Oh my God!"

"Get hold of yourself, Cathy! Try to relax. Everythin' will be alright, and there's plenty of time to get you to the hospital. You ain't feelin' no labor pains yet, are ya?"

"Well, I'm a little crampy and my tummy is starting to spasm. However, I don't know what labor pains feel like, Grandma."

"They'll probably be comin' on soon, and you'll know when you get 'em. Be sure to tell me when you do. I'll have Grandpa call the doctor. It may still be a while, and he can get the truck ready in the meantime. I'll pack you a bag, too, so we'll be all ready to go."

The labor pains started, then gradually intensified. The doctor had told Grandpa that we could wait until contractions were less than five minutes apart. It was early Christmas morning by the time we were on our way.

"Geez! The baby wants to come today so it can celebrate Christmas with us," Grandpa remarked.

I was lying down in the back seat, but could see him glance over at Grandma with a look of concern.

"I don't think we're going to make it to the hospital. Please HELP ME! I fear the baby is ready right now!" I cried out.

I was scared and was trying to hold back from pushing, but the pain was constant and intense.

"Lord Almighty! Ol' Man, you'd better find us a place to pull over and quick! There ain't no more time. Looks like you're gonna be deliverin' Billy and Cathy's child."

"I've delivered calves, but I've never done nothin' like this before. How can I be sure it'll come out okay?"

"It's gonna hafta, 'cause there ain't no other way!"

Grandpa immediately pulled to the side of the road while I continued to cry out. It hurt like hell.

As soon as he came around and opened the back door, I couldn't resist any longer. Grandpa hurried to lift my dress and remove my panties.

"I ain't meanin' to get so personal, Cathy, but this baby sure is in a rush. Look, Grandma, there's its head! Now what do I do?"

Grandma was standin' behind him, lookin' over his shoulder. "You do the same thing you did with our cow when she gave birth. Be ready to take hold of the little one when it comes out. Now, Cathy, let's have one big push and give it all you've got."

As I did, the baby slid right into Grandpa's big hands. His face lit up. "It's a boy!" he exclaimed.

Tears ran down my face. I wanted to hold my son right away, however, I was in total distress. "I'm still having painful contractions, Grandma. Is this normal?"

"You're passin' the placenta, but that shouldn't hurt. Everythin' looks okay, too. Grandpa's gonna cut and tie the cord next."

"But something's wrong. It feels like the baby's still in me. Help! I've got to push some more!"

Hmm, Ol' Woman, hold onto our grandson for a minute, so I can take a look. . . Sweet Jesus! There's another head a peekin' through. Congratulations, y'all, there's gonna be two!"

****

BILL

"Hurrah! C'mon, Commandos. Let's go meet Bob Hope at Bien Hoa Air Force Base. Colonel Rose gave me his permission yesterday; it's a surprise for y'all. He told me that Bob was bringin' Anita Bryant, Jill St. John, Maria Alberghetti, and Janis Paige, among others, as his special guests. Wow! I betcha they'll be some whoopin' and hollerin' by the troops, don't ya think? Of course, as for myself, I'll see Cathy up on that stage, wavin' to me, then sayin' "I have a Christmas surprise for you, Honey! So hurry home."

"Kinda miss Cathy and the baby, huh, Bill?"

Love Long Distance

"Like bees miss honey, Larry! Now, it's time to say, 'Po Bill,' get a seat close to the stage, then wait for the show to begin. Geez! Just look at 'em packin' in."

Bob Hope introduced the group; the applause was louder than bombs a burstin' in air. Then, someone yelled, "Shake it, Baby, 'cause I've got cream for the topping!" Why was I not smilin' and singin' happy songs? Why was I not back home with Cathy and our baby where I belonged?

The show was great, but I couldn't wait to get back to bed, lay down my head, and dream of bein' with her. The song, 'Christmas is the Time to be with Your Baby" kept playin' in my mind as I said my prayers and drifted off to sleep.

My dreamin' was sweet. I saw Cathy and me strollin' through the meadow, then sittin' beneath the willow tree. The butterflies were playin', "Catch me if you can," as they fluttered high into the sky to do whatever they do up there. The birds were singin' like church bells ringin'. Cathy smiled at me, winked, then asked, "Will you love me forever and ever, Honey?"

"Oh, yes! I'll love you that long, plus an extra day, too, Darlin'. Here's a poem I've

written from my soul, through my heart, by
my hand, for you, Beautiful.

TODAY, TOMORROW, AND FOREVER

Every moment we have spent together
has touched our lives, our souls forever.
The things we both have shared and
learned,
together multiply the love we've earned.

The person that I've grown into today,
did not get there by chance—no way!
I am who I am partly because of you,
and you are you because of me too.

The changes in yourself that you now see,
and what I have come to know about me,
are responses to how we carry our lives,
and what we discover in each other's
eyes.

No matter what happens, this much is
certain—
after life shuts down and closes its
curtain,

we'll remain as soulmates forever and a
day,
'cause not even death can get in Love's
way.

Tick-tock goes the clock!
*Please God, let me catch the train that's
gonna carry me home!*

****

"Is your name Bill from Pigeon Forge,
Tennessee, Commando?"

I opened my eyes to see a uniformed
man I didn't know with a serious
expression on his face. Immediately, I was
awake and sat up straight.

"It is!" I replied. "Why?"

"I'm here to deliver an urgent message
from your grandpa asking that you contact
him immediately."

"Thank you, Sir, and who are you?" I
tried not to appear worried, but I was.

"I'm Air Force Intelligence. Please come
with me. I'll take you to our telephone, so
you can make your call. Oh, and by the way
. . . Merry Christmas."

"Well, I certainly hope it will be," I
replied, as I jumped outta bed.

****

"Grandpa! What's a matta'? Our Intelligence Agent said it was urgent."

"First, let me say, Congratulations, Billy! You are the father of twins—a boy and a girl. However, the baby girl is currently in an incubator with undeveloped lungs. We don't yet know if she's gonna make it."

"Oh my God! She's gotta! Is Cathy okay?"

"That's the second part. Cathy's okay, but beside herself with worry. The doctor has contacted the American Red Cross and recommended they get you home fast. Grandma and I will do everythin' we can to help. Of course, you know this, don't ya?"

"You betcha! I'm headed for the Red Cross office here. Give my love to all, Grandpa."

As I hurried there, I trembled and prayed. *"Once again, You put the cross on my back, Father! It's gettin' so heavy—I can't bear it alone anymore. Please take my hand and help me, so I can best help Cathy and our little twins. For, after all,*

Love Long Distance

we're Your children! I'm waitin' on You, God. Please don't take long!"

CHAPTER 31

~ DREAMS COME TRUE ~

BILL

I walked into the Red Cross office and exclaimed, "Help me! I'm Bill—Commando Bill, and my boss is Colonel Rose, Commander of Commando Operations in Saigon, South Vietnam."

"Relax, Bill. Your boss is flying here, picking you up, then flying you home. We've already contacted him. He said to tell you that plans have changed and he'll brief you on the plane."

"God bless you, Sir. May I sit here and wait in this chair?"

"It will be an honor, Hero!"

****

I immediately rose from the chair and stood at attention when he arrived. He smiled as soon as he saw me, gave me a smart salute, then asked, "Is that one good enough, Commando, or should I go practice in the mirror?"

"Hello, Boss. The salute was acceptable, but your shoes need shinin'!"

"Hey, cut me some slack please! C'mon Bill, and bring along your motion sickness pills 'cause we gotta fly high into the sky, get on home, then have some of your Grandma's Smoky Mountain cherry pie."

"Well I'll be! With that Smoky Mountain talkin' you're a doin', I'd reckon you were from Tennessee, Colonel Rose!"

"Just practicing for the trip, Mountain Man. We've got a lot of talking to do along the way, and I want you to understand me loud and clear."

"Hmm . . . why do I feel there'll be no happy songs on the plane, Boss?"

"No questions now. Like I said, 'it's time to go.'"

Before we left, Colonel Rose gave another smart salute to the supervisor on duty, then told him, "Please tell the Red

Cross in Pigeon Forge to inform Bill's family that we're leaving Saigon now and are on our way. I'll be sure to send some kudos down channels thanking you all for your outstanding support. Merry Christmas and God Bless."

****

"This is your Captain, Heroes. Buckle up—I'm rollin'," announced the pilot after we boarded the plane.

"Captain, as soon as you reach cruising altitude, please tell us because we need to use the table for our work," Colonel Rose instructed.

Not long after takeoff, the Captain looked back quickly and said, "Colonel Rose, we have reached cruising altitude now."

"Thank you, Captain. Okay Bill, let's get started. The notepaper is in the rack — you're probably going to need it."

"Let me get my thinkin' cap on too, 'cause this sounds mighty important," I replied. "Course, I'm gonna have to fit it on tight to keep up with ya."

"Let's put that Smoky Mountain humor to bed for a little bit and listen up,

Commando. First off, effective as we speak, you are relieved of duty as the leader of my Joint Services Commando Team. Larry, your Navy Seal Master Instructor, will be taking your place."

"Shee! This is serious, Boss! I signed up to serve my country and that's what I plan to do, so what are ya gonna assign me to instead?"

"First of all, I am granting you a 30-day emergency leave to be with your family. You deserve to enjoy some time with Cathy and the twins. After your leave, you are to manage the transport of eight fallen war heroes from the Embassy of the United States in Saigon to the Arlington National Cemetery in Virginia. You shall, as well, plan and manage the burial ceremony. Long-term plans will soon be determined, but you won't get those orders until later. Now, do you feel that is acceptable, Commando?"

"Of course! My family is gonna be thrilled to have me close to home and outta that war zone for a time. I'll even be able to go fishin' with Grandpa—you betcha! If I may ask, Colonel Rose, what can I do to repay you for your kindness?"

"You can shine my shoes!"

"I'll take a raincheck on that if you don't mind, for after all, they actually look okay for a Boy Scout."

For the remainder of our flight, we played Blackjack poker, ate when we serviced the aircraft, and tried to look important. The boss arranged for a staff car once we landed at McGee Tyson Airport, near Knoxville. We shaved, showered, and took a three-hour nap at the National Guard facility there, then headed out. Before leavin', I called Grandpa.

"It's Billy. I'm in Blunt County. I'll be at the hospital within the hour. How are Cathy and our twins?"

"Cathy's heaps better and your son's doin' fine. As for your baby girl, she's not out of the woods yet; only time will tell. The doctor is a smart man; he's doin' everythin' he can."

"Tell Cathy I'm prayin' hard, and I'll be there soon. Tell her as well, that I love her and our babies, heart and soul. "

"Will do, Billy. Travel safe and God bless ya!"

Once we arrived at the hospital, Colonel Rose stopped after enterin' and said, "You need a little time alone with your family.

Why don't I go to the cafeteria and get me a cup of coffee while you visit?"

"Okay, Boss, but be sure to come by afterwards 'cause I want to introduce you to everyone," I replied.

"Promise, Bill. Now, get yourself there—and that's an order!"

I found my way to the maternity ward. When I entered Cathy's room, I saw her propped up in bed, readin' a book. I stood in the doorway marvelin' at how beautiful she was. Once catchin' sight of me, she smiled and exclaimed. "Well hello there, handsome new daddy. We've been waiting for you! Now get on over here and give me a kiss."

"Where are our babies?" I asked.

"They still need incubators, and visiting is limited; soon a nurse will take us to see them in the nursery ICU."

I walked over and sat on the edge of the bed. I kissed Cathy deeply and breathed in the sweet scent of her before sayin', "Please tell me more about our little girl. Is she gonna be okay?"

"Honey, we just got to keep on praying and believing that dreams come true. Our daughter was born with a condition called hyaline membrane disease. It's rare and usually happens in premature male babies, but also can occur in the second born of premature twins."

The technical term was scary to hear, and I knew I'd heard it before. Where that was, I couldn't be sure. This shouldn't be—did my family carry a curse? I pushed that thought from my mind. No, she was right—we had to keep prayin' and believin' everythin' would be alright.

"Where are Grandpa and the others anyway?" I asked. "I told them I was comin', so I expected they'd be here too."

"They'll be here a little later. I told them to wait a while. We have something to do before they arrive."

"See our babies, right? Where's that nurse then? I can't wait!" I knew I'd immediately fall in love with 'em.

"Well, I told her to leave us alone until I called for her. They're sleeping now and what we've got to do is just between me and you."

"Whippersnapper! Do you really think we should do it here in the hospital? Seriously? I'm not sayin' I don't wanna, but I thought you'd need some time to recover."

"I'm not believing my ears! I didn't mean THAT! No, Honey, we have to name our babies! I was thinking we might want to call our boy Billy, after you. Billy Junior— now doesn't that sound nice? Grandpa's already calling him his 'little man.'"

"That would be grand, Beautiful! Then why don't we call our girl Cathy, like you?"

"It'd be too confusing, Honey, because there's no such thing as a Cathy Junior. No, we've got to figure out another name."

"Hmm . . . I don't wanna say it, but what if she don't make it? Then she'll be a little angel of God just like . . ."

"I know . . . just like little Patrick Kennedy," Cathy replied. "God bless his sweet soul. How'd you know that was the same thing that gave him angel wings only two days after he was born in August of '63? But she's already lived longer than that, and we can't think that way. She's doing better every day, and weighs almost five pounds now—just one-half pound lighter than Billy. It's a good sign."

"Well I didn't know, but . . ." Suddenly it hit me. "That's it! We'll call her Angel, and she's made of strong chain. You betcha!"

Just then Grandpa and Grandma entered the room, followed by my boss.

"Great timing, everyone," Cathy said. "We just named our babies—Billy and Angel."

"Mighty fine names," Grandpa remarked. "Congratulations you two!"

"And since you're all here, now's a good time to also announce what Colonel Rose told me earlier," I said. "Better yet, I'll let him tell ya."

"Better than that!" replied Colonel Rose. "I got something to tell you all that YOU don't even know yet, Bill. I'll bet you'll be surprised."

CHAPTER 32

~ WELCOME HOME ~

BILL

"We are waitin' for the surprise, so c'mon let's hear it," Grandpa said.

"Yes, I'd love to hear what you have to say, Colonel Rose," Cathy added.

"Very well then. As I told Bill on the plane, I am granting him a 30-day emergency leave so he can spend some time with his family. After that he is to travel to Arlington National Cemetery to honor and pay tribute to eight fallen heroes, one of whom was the Navy Seal who died in his arms."

"That special assignment is an honor, Boss," I replied. I was anxious to hear what I was gonna do next.

"What I haven't told you, Bill, is that although we are still working on the details, you're not returning overseas. Instead, there is a top secret tactical project that you're being assigned to."

Cathy's eyes went wide. "Am I hearing you right, Colonel Rose?"

"Yes, Cathy. I am happy to say that this Smoky Mountain Man you love will be safely stationed stateside for the remainder of his active duty. Therefore, you can rest assured that Bill's got a good chance of living to see Billy and Angel grow up."

"Thank you for all you do," Grandma told him. "Just so you know, we're expectin' you to come 'round for supper before you head on back."

"That would be a pleasure. Thank you, Ma'am. May I ask what you're serving for dessert?"

"Why certainly!" Grandma remarked. "Billy told us your favorite, so we're havin' cherry pie!"

I looked over at Colonel Rose, then at Grandpa real quick. They had smiles longer than miles on their faces, and at the same time, we all replied, *"Goody, Goody!"*

****

My 30-day leave has just about rode off on a breeze, yet the timin' is good. Angel had to spend longer in the hospital, but she's now fine and where she belongs: home with the rest of us. Hurrah!

Yay! Today I'm gonna steal Cathy away from Grandpa and Grandma. While they watch the twins, we're gonna have a high ol' time in the meadow. I have our blanket in the pack to lie on the soft grass, then I'm plannin' to share with her a true story beginnin' with the day I was born.

****

CATHY

After we settled on the blanket and were enjoying the sights and sounds in the meadow, Bill said, "I gotta share somethin' with you. Are you listenin', Darlin'?"

"Of course, Handsome. What's the matter? You look so serious all of a sudden."

"That's because it's somethin' my family don't like to talk about. We've all tried to cast it out of our minds 'cause it brings us such sorrow. Grandma says it don't make much sense to stir up the past, yet we have been blessed with beautiful twins, and you have a right to know."

Bill reached in his pocket and pulled out a piece of white-lined paper. He unfolded it, then looked over at me and went on. "This is a true story I wrote when I was a teenager. I found it in the book of my writin's Grandpa still keeps. I figure readin' it to you might be the best way to tell ya, so here goes."

He cleared his throat, hesitated for a moment, then started . . .

Written by Billy (age 13)
GOD'S LITTLE ANGEL

The day my momma had me, she had another—my brother! His name was Bobby. Although we were not identical twins, we were as close as two peas in a pod and in many ways alike.

The years passed fast, and we celebrated our seventh birthday. As a gift, Grandpa gave us fishin' rods and said, "Go out to the river, fish from the bridge, and catch a heap for God's little angels because the Golden Pond is almost bare."

So, off we go—how many will we catch? Only God knows!

Bobby ran ahead, jumped upon the bridge rail, cast out his line, lost his balance then fell into the river.

"Please God! Don't take me yet, because Billy's heart would fall apart."

"Where are you, Bobby? Please wait, 'cause I'm jumpin' in and comin' to you!"

"Too late, Billy! I'm in Heaven, catchin' whoppers for our little angels! When you join me—bring your pole."

Bobby's body was never found. Three weeks later, I placed his picture in a coffin, then we buried it in the meadow under a big oak tree. He had told me earlier, "That's where I wanna be . . . when Jesus comes for me!"

I was speechless as I tried to hold back the tears. My heart was aching, almost breaking, for Bill. I knew that seeing our own Angel struggle to stay alive this past month made the memory of Bobby harder, not only for him, but also for his momma, Grandpa and Grandma.

"I'm sorry, Darlin'! I should have told you so much earlier. When I found out about Angel, I thought we carried a curse when it came to twins."

My eyes were filled with tears. "Aww, Honey, I'm the one who's sorry. You sharing with me like that just makes me love you more." I held and hugged him tight. "Both our babies are going to be all right!"

We sat on the blanket quietly for a while, still wrapped in each other's arms. The birds chirped in the trees, while the little squirrels scampered about. God's beauty was all around.

I finally stood up, stretched and said, "Tomorrow you'll be leaving for Arlington, so let's go home and love up Billy and Angel. But, before we do, I reckon you might want to love me up too. So, 1-2-3, I bet you can't catch me!"

Bill chased me across the meadow, and I've got to say, it wasn't long before I stopped running.

****

BILL

I said goodbye to all, climbed into the plane, then fell asleep. The time passed fast like a greyhound dog on the track, and I awoke in Arlington, Virginia.

My assignment there was to go to the National Cemetery and manage the burial of those eight war heroes. All were flown in from the Embassy of the United States in Saigon in South Vietnam. One of the eight was Mark.

I quickly chose a "Joint Services Color Guard" from the surroundin' units, then we were ready for the services to begin.

I stood tall and proud to be an American as the Color Guard marched to the memorial, made ready their weapons, then did the 21-gun salute. When Taps was sounded, I passed Ol' Glory to the next of kin of our dead. As I looked along the headstones of our heroes, I seemed to hear a whisper from above, *"Welcome home, My children!"*

After the dedication, Colonel Rose handed me an envelope and said, "Wait to open it with Cathy."

"Yes, Sir," I replied with a salute.

I bid my farewells, climbed aboard the plane and headed back to Tennessee. I tried sleepin'; yet when I closed my eyes, I saw Mark dyin' in my arms.

Once I got home, the demons kept runnin' wild in my mind. They've since disappeared for the most part, and I'm still here today to say, *"THANK YOU, FATHER!"*

CHAPTER 33

~ LOOKIN' BACK ~

BILL

Oh yes! I have walked through the fires in the pits of hell. I've stumbled and fallen, yet picked myself up to fight on. Through the blood and guts of it all—I stood tall . . . and did it God's way! I remember crystal clear, the year was 1961. At John F. Kennedy's Inaugural Address on January 20th he said, *"Ask not what your country can do for you, ask what you can do for your country!"*

Now the hurtful yesterdays are gone and I'm home. Of course there are times that demons return to my mind; but I pull them out and toss 'em back to hell from which they came.

Today I stole away to the meadow, and found myself lookin' back along the journey that Cathy and I have walked joined at the hip, as our hearts beat as one.

****

The sight of Cathy waitin' for me when I came home from Virginia remains in my memory, even though it was so many years ago. With both little Billy and Angel in her arms, she ran to me, and we embraced. With tears in our eyes, we looked down at our children. I thanked God I had gotten out of Vietnam alive, although I would continually ask Him, *"Why Mark and not me?"*

Strollin' together through the meadow, we rested in our favorite spot. That's when I pulled out the envelope from my boss and told Cathy it contained my next orders. I opened it and read the note inside:

Commando (aka Mountain Man),

It is with pleasure that I inform you that for the remainder of your active duty, you are being assigned to Sewart Air Force Base near Nashville, TN. There you will serve as US Commando Advisor and Intelligence. Further details about when to report for duty will be forthcoming soon. In the meantime, spend a little more time with Cathy and the twins.

Please thank your Grandma once again for that delicious supper, including the cherry pie. Also thank your Grandpa, although privately, for the moonshine he slipped me when Grandma wasn't looking.

It is an honor to give you this news. Congratulations and God Bless.

Respectfully,

Colonel A. Rose

Cathy put her head on my shoulder, and with a sigh of relief said, "I'm grateful we no longer have to be in love long distance."

****

Our "official" weddin' took place the followin' spring when the children were just beginnin' to walk. Butterflies fluttered about, the sun shone bright, and the Great Smoky Mountains in the foreground made for a majestic sight. Cathy wore a beautiful sundress that Grandma made special for the ceremony, and held onto a bouquet of fresh cut daisies. Grandpa walked her to me as I stood there in front of the minister. I was wearin' my uniform adorned with all of my medals. My Navy Seal, Larry, servin' as Best Man, was by my side. Cathy's cousin, Sue, was Maid of Honor, and both of our mommas, as well as Colonel Rose, were nearby lookin' on. Other family members, friends and neighbors were there also to share this blessin' from God.

We stood near this willow tree where we would recite poetry, and where our kids were conceived, as we said our vows to each other. Afterwards the minister declared us man and wife. I kissed Cathy, then for the grand finale, hand-in-hand, we both yelled out "HURRAH" and jumped over Grandma's broom.

Grandma had arranged for a wonderful picnic to follow. With red and white tablecloths laid out like patchwork in the meadow, we all gathered round, sat down, and enjoyed country fried chicken, cabbage apple slaw, butter smothered biscuits, and lemonade. A delicious Tennessee Mountain Stack Cake was dessert. Nothin' could've made this special day any better.

As Billy and Angel got bigger, Grandma fussed over them, and Grandpa enjoyed takin' them both fishin' as soon as they could hold a pole and bait a hook. They loved their great grandparents, and we lived right beside them in a log cabin of our own.

Time passed, and so did the days of our lives. Each day became sweeter than honey in a beehive. All at once, the sweet taste turned sour and the inevitable happened. Grandma climbed the stairway to Heaven, and Grandpa followed a week later.

As did David, a young Israelite teenager who slew Goliath, Billy grew into a man. Followin' in my footprints, he entered the Air Force, became a commando, and served 30 years of active military duty. He now lives not far away with his own family in South Carolina.

Angel grew up healthy and fine, and took a different path. Dolly Parton was her idol, so she picked up the guitar at a young age and also sang in the church choir. Once she turned 18, she headed on up to Nashville to the Grand Ol' Opry and became a star. It's always nice to see her beautiful face when she comes and visits after travelin' from place to place.

The Vietnam War hadn't taken my life like both Cathy and I feared it might. As we grew old together, Cathy continued to worry she might someday have to live without me, but that wasn't in God's master plan. He must've heard her pleas 'cause I wasn't the one who left this earth first—it was she. Cathy succumbed to cancer at the age of 73.

"Please bury me under the willow tree," she asked me on the last day of her life. She also said, "I love you deeply, and I thank you for our wonderful life together. We've been blessed in so many ways, and nothing, not even death, will ever break us apart. Until we are joined again in heaven, you'll always find me in your heart."

****

As I stand here by Cathy's grave, dressed in the same uniform I wore at our weddin', I recall the followin' poem I had written and recited to her only months before.

DEDICATED TO AN ANGEL OF GOD—MY WIFE

~ SOMEDAY ~

Someday I'll gather moonbeams that reflect in your eyes,
and forever keep them in my heart as a grand prize.
I'll collect rays of sunshine so golden bright,
to warm your lovin' heart on a cold winter's night.

Someday I'll capture the rainbow with a pot of gold,

then the sky will brighten as its beauty
unfolds.
Wherever you shall look, despite dark
clouds and rain,
it will banish sad thoughts and all our
earthly pain.

Someday I'll catch butterflies and put
them in a jar,
so I can sprinkle them on you to shine like
David's star.
The stormy wind will end, gently blowin'
as a breeze
that will so softly whisper, "I Love You,"
through the trees.

Someday we'll eat supper with Jesus and
drink a glass of wine,
before joyfully leavin' the earthly
yesterdays behind.
White capped waters of the ocean shall
rise and fall at times;
Yet I'll hold you warm and safe, your body
next to mine.

Someday I'll do all of these things for
you—plus more,
then forever together, Heaven we'll
explore.

Love Long Distance

Throughout eternity, our hearts will beat
as one.
True Love knows no distance and shall
never be undone."

****

"Our Long Distance Journey began with a
single step toward one another;
yet when our final earthly moment
neared, we reached and touched the
Face of God."

~The End~

~ A SALUTE! ~

Reflecting back I can see crystal clear the year, month, and day that I asked the Commander at Army Depot in Anniston, Alabama, for a tank to help erect a war memorial in the Panhandle of Florida in Marianna. He replied, "Ask and you shall receive; yet you will have to fill out enough paperwork to feed a hungry goat for a year. Then it'll have to be approved by headquarters before I can release it to you, Bill. Do you still want it, Bishop?"

"Of course I do! Yet I'll have to go and buy a goat!" I replied.

The month to follow would change my life forever. On the way home, I stopped at a veterans' cemetery. As I approached the resting place of our war dead, I stood tall, chin up, chest out, proud and called, "A 'SALUTE' to all our heroes across America!"

Quickly kneeling, I prayed. "May the patriotism, raw courage, and fighting spirit of our warriors having died in the folds of Ol' Glory be chiseled in our hearts forever."

After finishing my speech at the memorial dedication, I stepped down from the podium, then seemed to hear a whisper saying, *"Well done, My son. I go to prepare a place for all My children."*

Glory, Glory, Hallelujah! No more *Rat-a-tat-tat—Kaboom—Kaboom!*

Respectfully,

Bill Bishop

~ REFERENCES ~

Following is a list of some of the most notable references within this novel.

◇ Lackland Air Force Base, San Antonio, Texas

◇ Beatles' first performance on the Ed Sullivan Show – February 9, 1964

◇ Heavyweight Champion fight between Sonny Liston and Cassius Clay – February 25, 1964

◇ Eglin Air Force Base is located in Western Florida, approximately three miles southwest of Valparaiso in Okaloosa County

◇ Buck Owens – *"My Heart Skips a Beat"*

◇ Elizabeth Taylor's marriage to Richard Burton – March 15, 1964

◇ James Francis (Jimmy) Durante – American actor, comedian, singer and pianist – active from 1920-1972

◇ The Dave Clark Five – *"Glad All Over"*

◇ Issuance of the Kennedy Half Dollar

◇ Five-Star General Douglas MacArthur –

died on April 5th, 1964

◇ Old (Ol') Glory – Nickname for the flag of the United States. The original "Old Glory" was a flag owned in the 19th century by William Driver, an American sea captain.

◇ Temple Houston – NBC television series 1963/64

◇ Marvin "Popcorn" Sutton – American Appalachian moonshiner/bootlegger

◇ Bobby Vinton – *"There I've Said It Again"*

◇ Alabama Crimson Tide (University of Alabama football team) – Joe Namath (QB 1962-1964); Bear Bryant (Head Coach 1957-1982)

◇ *Cat's Cradle* – a novel by Kurt Vonnegut (1963)

◇ Grand Ole Opry, Nashville, Tennessee

◇ Uncle Jimmy (Jessie Donald) Thompson – an American old time fiddle player and singer/songwriter

◇ Nashville's first "instant park" (former Maxwell House site)

◇ Actress Joan Crawford at Beamon

Bottling Company, Nashville, TN – April 26, 1964

◇ Evangelist Oral Roberts at Nashville's Municipal Auditorium – April 23-26, 1964

◇ Civil rights demonstration on West End Avenue, Nashville, TN – April 27, 1964

◇ Louis Armstrong – *"Hello, Dolly"*

◇ Assassination of President John F. Kennedy – November 22, 1963 – Dallas, Texas

◇ Tennessee Psychiatric Hospital and Institute - Memphis

◇ *One Flew Over the Cuckoo's Nest,* a novel by Ken Kesey (1962)

◇ Amazing Grace – written in 1772 by John Newton; hymn published in 1779

◇ Cliff Hess – *"Blue Ridge (Mountain) Blues"*

◇ Cherokee Indian Reservation is located in Cherokee, North Carolina

◇ Johnny Cash – *"I Walk the Line"*

◇ Walter Cronkite, CBS News Anchor from 1962 to 1981

◇ Jim Reeves – *"Adios Amigo"*; Jim died

in a plane crash on July 31, 1964. His body was found two days later.

◇ Roger Miller – *"Chug-a-Lug"*

◇ Gulf of Tonkin Incident – President Lyndon Johnson's Vietnam Address on August 4, 1964

◇ Patsy Cline – *"Crazy"*

◇ Daisy Girl – President Lyndon Johnson's controversial re-election ad

◇ Greenwich Village, New York, NY

◇ Howard Johnson's Restaurant was founded by Howard Deering Johnson- it was the largest chain restaurant in the U.S. throughout the 1960s and 1970s

◇ Elvis Presley – *"All Shook Up"*

◇ Tennessee Country Pride Sausage – this food brand originated in the Nashville area in 1943

◇ Elvis Presley – *"Burning Love"*

◇ Winchester Level-Action Rifle, designed by John Browning in 1894, became one of the most famous and popular hunting rifles of all time

◇ Hurricane Cleo – a Cat. 2 that made landfall in Miami, Florida, on August 27,

1964

◇ General Hospital – ABC Soap Opera (4/1/1963-Present)

◇ McDonald's Restaurant – by 1964, there were approximately 1000 McDonald's Restaurant locations. At that time, a hamburger cost 17 cents

◇ Tyndall Air Force Base is located 12 miles east of Panama City, Florida

◇ Captain Anderson's, Panama City Beach, Florida – this restaurant was originally owned by brothers, Max and Walter Anderson in 1960. It was sold in 1967 after Captain Walter Anderson's death

◇ Snake-a-torium – owned by Dennie Seabolt. It was the first tourist attraction in Panama City Beach, Florida (1936-1991)

◇ Ross Allen's Jungle Shows, Panama City Beach, Florida (1963-1965)

◇ Miracle Strip Amusement Park, Panama City Beach, Florida – originally founded in 1964 by Ed Neilson

◇ The Hang Out - Beginning in the 1940's, it was the most popular place to "hang out" in Panama City Beach, Florida. Hurricane Eloise damaged it beyond repair in 1975.

◇ Tan Son Nhut Air Base (1955-1975) – Republic of Vietnam Air Force Base facility located in Saigon

◇ Bien Hoa Air Base – South-Central Southern Vietnam – In the early 1960s, this became a joint operating base for both the RVNAF and USAF. The Americans used this as a major base during the Vietnam War from 1961-1973

◇ Francis Scott Key – *"The Star Spangled Banner"* – September 14, 1814 (poem) – it was later set to music and became America's National Anthem in 1931

◇ Harry Houdini – Hungarian-born American Illusionist and Stunt performer from 1891-1926

◇ David Glasgow Farragut was an accomplished U.S. naval officer, most known for his service to the Union during the American Civil War

◇ 1964 Presidential Election – On November 3rd, President Lyndon B. Johnson (Dem) was re-elected, defeating Barry Goldwater (Rep. nominee) by 61.1% of the vote

◇ Viet Cong Assault at Bien Hoa AFB – Viet Cong mortar attack; four American dead and 72 wounded

◇ Typhoons, South and North Vietnam – Early November, 1964 – Typhoon Iris, followed closely by Typhoon Joan, temporary halted most combat operations and caused over 5000 deaths

◇ The Supremes – *"Baby Love"*

◇ Annual Bob Hope Christmas Show – Bien Hoa Air Base, Vietnam – December 24, 1964 - approximately 1000 airmen were in attendance

◇ The Orchids – *"Christmas Is The Time To Be With Your Baby"*

◇ Embassy of The United States in Saigon (1962-1975)

◇ Arlington National Cemetery. Arlington County, Virginia – the country's largest military cemetery

◇ McGee Tyson Airport, Alcoa, Tennessee – located in Blount County, near Knoxville

◇ Hyaline Membrane Disease – a respiratory disease of the newborn, usually when born prematurely – now called Respiratory Distress Syndrome (RDS)

◇ Patrick Bouvier Kennedy (August 7, 1963 - August 9, 1963) – Infant child of President John F. Kennedy and First Lady Jacqueline Kennedy. Born prematurely, he died of Hyaline Membrane Disease

◇ 21-gun salute – customary gun salute performed by the fire of cannons or artillery as a military honor; is the highest honor rendered

~ ABOUT THE AUTHORS ~

Bill Bishop, co-author, was born in the Smoky Mountains of Tennessee. After formal education, he served 30 years active duty with the U. S. Air Force, then relocated to the Panhandle of Florida. He is quick to say, *"I love America, baseball, and apple pie!"*

~ ~ ~

Cathy Waldron, co-author, is a native of New Hampshire. Her debut novel, *in Polyester Pajamas*, won the NH Writers' Project 2013/2014 Readers' Choice Award for outstanding work of fiction. She's thrilled to now be co-authoring with Bill Bishop.